"You're going to h seat, Nicky."

"Okay," she quipped see him, hear his voice from there. She started toward her chair.

"Not just yet, though," he said, grabbing her wrist. His hand was large and warm, just as she knew it would be. And without even closing her eyes she knew what it would feel like to have his hands on her body. He would be tender, his touch gentle, but his kisses would be filled with an intensity that stole her breath away. She felt her body tighten in hunger and she turned toward him. She wanted that kiss, wanted that caress. She wanted him more than she'd ever wanted anything in her life.

"Before you go back," he was saying, "I'm going to count to three. When I finish, you're going to wake up and remember everything you've done here with a happy glow."

She laughed. He was being ridiculous. Because Nicky had no intention of leaving this warm, wonderful, sexy place.

Ever.

Blaze

Dear Reader,

I recently went on a cruise and had the absolute best time! Mostly I read and ate. There might even have been drinking involved! And one night, I attended a hypnotist's show. It was hilarious! My daughter's friend turned out to be highly suggestible. Though normally a shy young man, he was suddenly Michael Jackson dancing "Thriller," complete with sparkling glove and pelvic thrusts. It was one of the funniest things I've ever seen. It was also inspiring.

What if a woman was on the verge of a breakdown? What if that exhausted, stressed-out woman named Nicky got hypnotized by a stage act...?

That's why this book is one of the FORBIDDEN FANTASIES. Nicky's sudden lack of inhibition opens the door to all sorts of interesting scenarios. Fortunately she has the perfect man to help her. Jimmy Rayburn has loved Nicky since high school. And he's especially skilled at creating safe, sexy and downright mesmerizing environments to prove that he is just the man for her.

Hope you enjoy my walk on the wild side. I certainly did!

Kathy Lyons

Kathy Lyons

UNDER HIS SPELL

Get spellbound!
Kathy Lyons

HARLEQUIN®

TORONTO • NEW YORK • LONDON
AMSTERDAM • PARIS • SYDNEY • HAMBURG
STOCKHOLM • ATHENS • TOKYO • MILAN • MADRID
PRAGUE • WARSAW • BUDAPEST • AUCKLAND

Recycling programs
for this product may
not exist in your area.

ISBN-13: 978-0-373-79539-0

UNDER HIS SPELL

ABOUT THE AUTHOR

Kathy Lyons is a *USA TODAY* bestselling author... under a different name. As Jade Lee, she writes sexy historical romances. But Kathy Lyons is younger, hipper and a lot more fun than her history-loving counterpart. Kathy writes funny, contemporary books hotter than a cover model's hello! If you want to share which name is the better writer, please e-mail her at kathy@kathylyons.com. Or, if you insist, you can e-mail that other woman at jade@jadeleeauthor.com.

To Brenda Chin. Thank you for seeing the diamond under the dross. This book is special because of you. And to Pamela Harty, agent extraordinaire. Without you, this book never would have been at all. And best of all, to Amanda, who said, Hey Mom, I like cruises!

1

"DON'T FORGET, NICKY. Please, sis, you can't forget."

Nicky Taylor ground her teeth, then stopped, worried that her older sister, Susan, would hear it over the Bluetooth connection.

"What?" Susan asked. "What did you say?"

"Aieee!" Nicky swerved her car, then slammed on the brakes as she tried to avoid a motorcycle zipping too fast down the oncoming lane. No less than three other cars had to do something similar, and their horns blared angrily all around her.

"Damn cyclists!" she cursed even as she flushed in embarrassment. Truthfully, that near-accident had been her fault. She'd been trying to maneuver around a slow-moving bus. She was in a section of Chicago that had the triple threat: narrow lanes, heavy traffic and three streets intersecting in a confusing mess.

"Nicky! Nicky, are you all right?"

"Yes, yes," she groused to cover her own guilt. "I'm meeting Tammy at that club and I'm late."

"You're always late. What happened?"

"Nothing, nothing. Just a motorcyclist and a city bus."

She glanced at the time and her chest tightened exponentially. Damn, she hated being late. "Tammy is going to have a fit. The first amateur act has probably already started."

"We're used to you being late. I'll text her that you're on your way. Just drive carefully, okay?"

Nicky winced, knowing that her reputation was well deserved. But she was building a career—didn't they understand that? "I'm not always late. And I drive just fine."

Susan's inelegant snort blasted through the line. "You drive fine when you're concentrating on it. When was the last time you tried to do one thing at a time?"

Nicky didn't answer. She was too busy straightening out her car behind the gawd-awful bus. At least with it going slowly, she'd be able to check her e-mails as soon as she got off the phone. Her company manufactured plastic containers. It wasn't rocket science, but they made *a lot* of containers. Unfortunately, the world was cutting back on its plastic consumption, which meant as regional head of five distribution nodes, Nicky had to find a way to scale back without firing hundreds of employees.

Part of her just wanted to throw in her resignation along with the layoffs. Shipping plastic parts around the country wasn't exactly what she'd planned when she received her MBA. She'd dreamed of making green products, of earning her living while saving the planet. Plastic was as far from that as she could have gotten. But they'd offered her money and a fast track to the executive boardroom. She hadn't counted on the hundred-hour workweek or the fact that she'd stall out in middle management while the economy took a serious downturn.

Fortunately her little sister, Tammy, knew a guy who

specialized in shipping optimization. That's who she was really meeting at amateur night. Nicky just prayed that Prof. Thompson could help her optimize without firing. But he'd have to look at the reports first, which had to be compiled from data from each division head, and then...

"Nicky? Are you still there?"

"Hmm?" She forcibly pulled her attention back to her sister. And the damn bus. And being late to see Prof. Thompson at some stupid amateur night, all before she looked at those figures from the East Coast factory. Her chest tightened further, and she had to force a deep breath. She would not have a panic attack here. Not while driving. No, no, *no!* She just needed a moment to breathe.

"Nicky?"

"Yeah, I'm still here," she said, still willing her breath to even out. "Still stuck. Stupid bus."

There was a picture on the back of the bus of a tropical resort. Nicky stared at it a moment, her thoughts wandering to a sandy beach and a hot guy rubbing oil on her back. Wouldn't that be heaven? She held on to the image for a moment, really savored it. It had been years since she'd been with a man. She'd been too busy, too focused, and too afraid of making another bad boyfriend choice. But in fantasy land, she could pretend anything. She could be on a hot beach with the absolute perfect man caressing her in the most intimate ways. It would be so good...

She held on to the thought, soaked it into her skin, and felt her breath lengthen. Moments later, her body relaxed enough for her to function. No panic attack. Life was good.

Except, of course, life wasn't good. She still was

nearly an hour late for her appointment, and even when she made it, she didn't have all the figures together. She didn't even see a time when she could take her island vacation. Not until the economy took a better turn. Not until…

"I've e-mailed you the dates…"

Nicky frowned. Dates for what? Oh yeah, her god-daughter's christening. There was a meeting with the priest and then the actual event. She just couldn't forget. "Thanks, Suz."

"Five o'clock Thursday with the priest, okay?"

Nicky nodded, her thoughts still wandering toward the tropical island and a hot guy with body oil. "Does it have to be at five?" She couldn't remember the last time she'd left work that early. Sun, sand, a man…

"You already said you could make it at five!"

"Okay, okay! Five o'clock Thursday."

"You just can't—"

"Can't forget, I know, I got it!" An ache cramped her belly painfully. It was stress. Duh. Her breath was getting short again, so she continued ranting because it felt good. And because it staved off the panic attacks that were getting more frequent with every passing day. "I manage five nodes, supervise nearly two thousand employees, and everyone thinks I can't remember a simple appointment with a priest!" She'd have to remember to put it in her phone calendar. With warnings three days in advance. But she couldn't do that while driving and talking on the phone.

"Nicky, honey, it's not that I don't think you're capable—"

"I know, I know. I gotta go. This bus is driving me nuts." Then she clicked off before her sister could argue.

With a grunt of frustration, she swiveled around in her seat, watching for a break in traffic and furious when she didn't see one. She knew she was overreacting. But she still had a ton of work to do without a clue about when she'd get it in. Who put amateur night on a Thursday, anyway? She should have said no, but she needed to consult Prof. Thompson. And, oh no, she still had to do her laundry. Did she have anything clean for tomorrow? Did she have time to buy some underwear on the way to the bar?

Her phone beeped with a text just as she was finally shifting to the next lane. The pressure built in her mind and body as she stopped her instinctive jerk to answer the phone. She was driving, damn it. Any text could wait!

She steadied the car and pushed through a light, but the cramp in her stomach returned as she ignored the message on her phone. What if it was her boss? What if one of the offices had trouble sending the report? It was well after seven, but she knew at least three of her immediate subordinates worked the same crazy hours she did. If it was one of them, then she needed to get on the problem right away. Jobs were on the line, hers included. She knew there was a way to save most of them, but she had a lot of work to do to find it.

With a grunt of disgust, she grabbed her phone and hit the appropriate button. It was awkward reading and driving at the same time, but she'd mastered it a long time ago. With a sigh of relief, she saw it was from her sister Tammy and not a work disaster.

Where r u?

She stopped at a light and whipped off a response.

Almost there! she texted. It was a lie, but if there were no more buses between her and the bar, she'd make it before the end of the second act. Unless another disaster hit. She tried not to think of that. She tried not to think of tropical islands either or the way her entire body clenched with frustration. If she could just get through the immediate crisis, she would deal with the rest later. But God, what she wouldn't give to be on that tropical island now....

JIMMY RAY DID a double take, jerking the curtain slightly as he peered out at the crowd. It couldn't be her. That absolutely could *not* be Nicky Taylor, his high school fantasy walking into the bar. She'd been a volleyball star, class president and the girl voted most likely to run the country in twenty years. And he'd wanted her forever. What was she doing here at amateur night?

He leaned forward, peering into the dimly lit crowd. He couldn't be sure it was her. Lots of women had long legs, gray business suits and that look of anxious harassment in their eyes. But only Nicky walked that way, with her hips shifting in a lilting cadence while her pointy chin dared a man to try for her. Could that really be her? The blond hair was right, but this woman had a tight lift to her shoulders that high school Nicky never had. She was also walking and trying to read on her BlackBerry while taking off her coat and scanning the crowd at the same time. That was vintage Nicky, even in high school. He bet she'd mastered multitasking by the time she was six.

He frowned as he watched the woman who might be Nicky reach her destination. There was another woman there nursing a margarita. He had to wait for a shift in the lights, but…yes! That was Tammy, Nicky's younger sister. He was sure of it. After all, he'd lived down the block from the Taylor family for years. He knew all of Nicky's family, had trick-or-treated at their house, had even shared a yearly Christmas potluck. He knew them the way he knew how to construct a saw-the-lady-in-half illusion. The woman at the table was Tammy, which meant the other woman—the blonde with the overstuffed briefcase—was Nicky Taylor. Here at amateur night. Of all the dumb luck!

Anticipation tightened his gut. Or was that fear? He closed his eyes, clenching his jaw in disgust. He'd gotten past the nausea that came with painful shyness the day he'd received his first six-figure check. He'd even forced himself up on stage at his brother's bar just to make sure he could overcome his fear of public speaking. But one look at Nicky's long legs in killer black pumps, and he was right back in high school complete with gut-churning panic. Back then he'd resorted to the fantasy of being a magician, of mesmerizing all in his path with his suave charm. Now he was a man and a millionaire. He did not need to hide in fantasy to talk to a woman. Even if that woman was Nicky Taylor, the girl who'd owned his heart since he was twelve.

He had to find a way to talk to her, to have that shot he'd missed in high school. But how? A dozen scenarios spun through his brain, each growing more far-fetched. In the end, he cut off his overactive reasoning. That had been his problem in high school: too much thinking and too little action. By the time he'd worked up the perfect plan to seduce Nicky Taylor, they'd already graduated and gone on to college. Tonight he would keep it simple.

He would magic her into his arms.

2

"AND NOW for my greatest trick..."

Nicky barely heard the magician's prattle. Her attention was focused on her latest e-mail as she hit Next Page on her phone. Professor Thompson was a no-show. Or rather, he'd shown but left when Nicky was late. Tammy hadn't told her, of course. Her little sister had this misplaced idea that Nicky needed some fun in her life. Well, duh. But sitting through amateur night at a bar didn't qualify. Unfortunately Tammy could be annoyingly insistent, so rather than cause a scene, Nicky had sat down, ordered some wine and promptly buried her nose in her e-mail. It was hard to see in the bar/theater, especially with the flickering flash explosions from the stage, but if she held the phone's screen about six inches from her nose, she could read well enough.

"I'm going to separate this woman from her phone!"

A hand shot out and swiped her BlackBerry right out of her palm.

"Hey!" Nicky cried out, then she had to blink against the glare of the spotlight. Laughter erupted all around her, most especially from Tammy, who waved her margarita in salute.

"Well, you were being rude," Tammy said as she winked at the magician.

Nicky acknowledged the hit with an apologetic shrug. "Sorry...umm—" her gaze slipped over to the stage display "—Magic Man." Was that really his act's name? "I apologize for saving my career during your magic act."

"That's all right. I always forgive beautiful women." The magician flashed her a killer, megawatt smile. This close up, she could see that he was quite the cutie, in a hometown, wholesome kind of way. Brown eyes, light brown hair, pale white skin. The stage lights weren't doing him any favors on that score. They seemed to highlight exactly how dark and mysterious he *wasn't*. And yet, she responded to him. An image of her island hottie flashed through her brain, and she found herself thinking that if this magician got a good tan and stepped into a short sarong, she could absolutely settle down in the sand next to him. The idea was so strong, her fingers actually itched to see what kind of muscles lay hidden under his tux.

But rather than fondle the main attraction right under the lights, she flashed her own version of a killer smile. "Thank you," she said, holding out her hand for her phone. "I promise I'll turn it off now."

"Hmmm, forgiveness is one thing. Property is something else entirely." He grinned as he started backing up to the stage, holding her phone hostage as he moved. "Would you care to join me onstage? Perhaps we can let you win your phone back."

Her fantasy reluctantly faded as her body began to clench. She needed that phone. Just the thought of all the things that could go wrong if she lost it had her close to hyperventilating. "No, no, no. I need that phone."

"Go on," encouraged Tammy from behind her margarita. "It'll be fun."

Nicky gave her sister a glare. Tammy's idea of fun was vastly different than her own.

Meanwhile, the Magic Man was beginning to flip through her e-mail. "Let's see what we have here. Work. Work. Sales info. Factory specs. Yawn." He dropped the phone in a top hat on his magician's table. "A beautiful woman shouldn't be that very boring. I can see why you don't want it back."

Nicky was already standing, her hand stretched out. "This isn't funny," she said, the constriction in her chest making her breath short and tight. "Please, take my sister. She's a lot more fun than me." It wasn't true of course, or it hadn't been true before college. She'd been loads of fun then. Why couldn't she breathe? "Please give me back my phone!"

"Too late!" Tammy quipped as she licked salt off the edge of her drink. "Phone's gone."

"No!" Nicky knew it was a trick. After all, this was a stage show. But her phone really was gone! The little magician's table was empty and the top hat with the phone inside was nowhere in sight. Terror clutched at her chest way out of proportion to the event. Her whole life was in that phone. What if something happened during his flashfire explosions? What if it dropped down a trapdoor and broke?

What if you never got it back, you couldn't do the work and you were forced to take the rest of the week off because of it?

She winced at that inner voice. She knew its seductive tones, knew it was the voice of her island hottie tempting her to the dark side. And for some bizarre reason, she put the magician's face on her fantasy man. But she couldn't do it. She had a job and responsibilities, though the sudden yearning for escape rolled through her mind like a sweet, hot wind. "I really need that back," she said, hating that her voice was strangled. "It's my life."

"Darling, your life has got to be more exciting than this phone," returned the Magic Man, his voice just as seductively tempting.

Let him have the phone. Let him have it all, her fantasy man whispered.

"I can't," Nicky breathed as her hands tightened into fists. She was at the base of the stage now, scanning it for any sign of her BlackBerry. "Just give me my phone back."

"I'll make you a deal," the Magic Man said, pitching his voice to the room at large. "If I can psychically guess your name, then you have to come up onstage and help me out."

Play with me. That's what he was saying to her. *Come play.* How she wanted to. Hot sun, hot oil, hot man. God, it hurt just thinking about it.

"I have to work, and you don't need to guess anything. My name's on my phone."

The Magic Man shook his head. "Your phone said N. Taylor and has a picture of your dog—"

"Actually," piped up her sister, "that's my dog."

He paused and frowned at Nicky. "That's not even your dog? Now, that is sad."

Nicky shot a glare at her sister as she climbed the steps onto the stage. "Did you set this up?"

Tammy shook her head. "Not guilty, I swear! Though I would have if I'd thought about it."

Nicky made it onstage, her mind at war with itself. Half of her kept putting that hot island man in place of the magician. The other kept shoving the image away, refusing to give in to her dreams even if it made her entire body clench in panic. Only by sheer force of will was she able to speak with anything like a normal tone. "Fine, Mr. Magic Man. I'm here. Guess my name, then give me back my phone."

"Oooh, a challenge." His voice was growing deeper and more mesmerizing. It perfectly fit her imagined island guy who kept whispering seductive fantasies in her mind. Then he touched her cheek. It was the barest caress, but it was definitely a caress, and her breath cut off completely. "Look into my eyes."

She bit her lip, making one last desperate attempt to keep it together. To keep her life together. "Please," she whimpered, "just give me back my phone."

"It's all right," he murmured. "Everything will be fine." Even knowing that everyone could hear what he said, Nicky felt as if his words were just for her. And they carried such power. A release. Sun. Hot oil. A man stroking her body. She nearly cried out at the lure of it all.

"Your real name is Charlotte, but you don't like it. You renamed yourself Nicky after Stevie Nicks because you always wanted her straight blond hair." He pushed his fingers into her hair, rubbing sweetly against her scalp as he released it from her heavy clip.

"You can't know that," she murmured, but obviously he did. And as the clip slipped off, her mind began to slip free. Inside she was a little closer to that tropical island. Just a little more, one tiny step more and soon she'd be running naked through the sand. It didn't make sense, but his voice made it seem so real.

"Just listen to my voice, Nicky. As long as you can hear my voice, you're safe. Do you understand, Nicky? You're always safe with me."

She felt it. At some core level, she felt that absolute peace that came with safety. With just his words and his voice, he made everything okay.

"This isn't possible," she said as she valiantly reached for sanity. But did she really want to return to the chains of endless statistics, boxes of plastics and layoffs? And all the while, his voice kept flowing over her. It felt hot and soothing, like the oil she imagined him stroking onto every part of her body.

"You weren't a cheerleader in high school," he said. "Volleyball team. Setter. But you really wanted to be a singer in a band."

"Like Stevie Nicks," she whispered. He knew everything about her.

She was still looking into his eyes. She couldn't look away even if her life depended on it. Brown eyes, brown hair, her rational mind tried to label him as ordinary and unimpressive. But that was a lie, just like everything about reality was a terrible lie. His face was kind, his eyes were a rich mocha, and his voice was the best of all because it created this place for her. He was her island god, and his voice made it real.

He was looking down at her, leaning in close. Would he kiss her? She wanted him to. With one kiss, she would be there with her island god. God, how she wanted it!

"Your senior night prom was a disaster," he said. "You wore a white Greek goddess gown, your date was an ass and you ended up walking part of the way home."

She winced, her eyes tearing at the remembered pain.

"Remember you're safe, Nicky. Nothing can hurt you here."

It was true. She felt it, and her mind slipped forward in time past that horrible disaster of a prom date to what had happened afterward. To her neighbor and school nerd Jimmy Ray who had found her as she was walking home. He'd taken her to an all-night diner and they'd eaten ice cream sundaes until she thought she would puke. They'd talked and laughed and shared a single kiss. It was fabulous, and whenever she thought of that night, she focused on those ice cream sundaes and that kiss.

"It was the best night of my life," she said.

"Really?" drawled the Magic Man. His eyes were frowning and that created a ripple of discontent in her island world. But she didn't have time to think about it as his expression smoothed and his voice returned to that deep, low timber. He made every word feel like hot oil stroking the tension out of her body. "Relax, Nicky. Let reality slip away. You are safe and free as you haven't been for years. No work. No responsibilities. Just rest, release and sweet—"

"Pleasure," she murmured. Then she took a deep breath, allowing herself to slide deeper into the fantasy. How glorious to let go of the tension and fear she had been holding. Her life had been spinning out of control for some time now. She felt like a mouse on a wheel that had jumped the tracks. She was inside it, running for all she was worth while her life careened to she-didn't-know-where. But she couldn't jump out and she couldn't stop. Until now. Until her island god extended his hand and led her step by step to paradise.

"Everything is fine, Nicky, as long as you're with me. I will keep you safe."

So true, she thought with a smile. His voice, his presence, was her way out of the spinning mouse wheel and she grabbed on to it with both hands. She opened herself to him, to his hot oil voice. He could touch her anywhere, pleasure her any way, and she would love it. She closed her eyes and felt her mouth slip open just a bit. She could taste the ocean on her tongue, feel the sand beneath her feet. She was free because *he* made it so.

She wanted to strip off her clothes and dance naked in the sand. She wanted to frolic with her island god. His words were like hands caressing her, his breath was the air that skated across her flushed skin. She was here in this place of wonder, and she was never, ever going to leave.

It was so easy. Like opening her hands and letting go. Reality slipped away, fantasy took root and wrapped her in such wonder.

"Do you feel it, Nicky? Freedom? Joy?"

"Safety," she whispered. "I can breathe again!" She took a deep breath, feeling oxygen flood her body like never before. It made her light-headed and so happy. As long as her island god was with her, everything was right. It was more than right. It was *perfect!*

"Do you want your cell phone back?"

"God, no."

"Sing for us, Nicky. Sing 'Never Going Back Again' just like Stevie Nicks."

No problem. In this place, she could do anything! She took the mike from his hand and began belting out the song. It was easy because it was true. She wasn't ever going back again. And then when she stopped singing, her island god came back to her side.

"That was amazing, Nicky. Now, I want you to see what I have in my hand here."

She looked. "It's my cell phone."

"Do you see what's over there?"

She frowned.

"It's a volcano. Do you see it, Nicky? The volcano right there?"

There it was! Right in the middle of the stage. Amazing! "Yes, of course I do."

"I want you to take your cell phone now and drop it into the volcano. Can you do that?"

A shiver of fear slid down her spine. There was a reason she shouldn't do that. Something important, but if she thought about it, then she'd have to leave this wonderful place. She'd have to leave *him*. And that was the last thing she wanted to do.

"Remember, Nicky, nothing bad can happen to you in this place. I'm with you here. You can let go of your phone and still be safe and happy."

Of course she could. She was with her island god. With a grin, she took her cell phone from him and danced over to the volcano. It felt great, so absolutely wonderful to do this. Then, easy as opening her hand, she let her cell phone go. It dropped away. Poof! Into the volcano, never to be seen again!

"How do you feel, Nicky?"

"Alive. So wonderfully alive!" Then she twirled around in a circle with her arms spread wide. She could breathe, she could dance, she could even sing! All because of him. "I want to stay here forever!"

He laughed, and she laughed with him. "I want to thank you for your help, Nicky. But it's time for you to go back to your seat now."

She frowned, but then she relaxed again. She could

still see him from her seat. She could even hear his voice from there. "Okay," she quipped as she started toward her chair.

"Whoa!" he cried as he grabbed her wrist. His hand was large and warm, just as she knew it would be. And without even closing her eyes she knew what it would feel like to have his hands on her body. He would be tender, his touch gentle, but his kisses would be filled with an intensity that stole her breath away. She felt her body tighten in hunger and she turned toward him. She wanted that kiss, wanted that caress. She wanted *him* more than she'd ever wanted anything in her life.

"Before you go back," he was saying as he held her hand, "I'm going to count to three. When I reach three, you're going to come back into yourself and remember everything you've done here with a happy glow."

She laughed, really laughed, because what he said was so ridiculous. She was herself here. She had never been *more* herself than right now in this safe place that he had created.

"Are you ready, Nicky? After I count to three, you'll be yourself and go back to your seat with a happy smile."

She nodded, but she didn't speak because she had a secret. She wasn't going to listen to him count. She was going to do exactly as he said, except for one thing. When he reached three, she wasn't going to leave this perfect place. She was safe here. If anything, by the time he reached three she was going to go deeper, submerge herself more completely, and become as wholly, perfectly herself as she could ever be!

"One," he began to count. "Two."

"Three!" she cried in concert with him, throwing up her arms in glee.

She saw his face flash with concern. Did he know? Did he guess that she was still in the wonderful place he had created?

"So, how do you feel, Nicky?" he asked.

She smiled. "I think I'll go sit down now." That was, after all, what he had said. After he counted to three, she would go back to her seat.

"Wonderful," he said. "No hard feelings?"

She shook her head. "No hard feelings at all." There was no room for anything that awful here.

"Great!" he said to the audience at large. Then he waggled his eyebrows. "And if you want to continue this later, just come by my house tonight. I'm listed in the phone book under Magic Man!"

The music hit her then with a crash of cymbals. The audience applauded and the lights flashed as Nicky made her way to her seat. Internally, she flinched away from all of that. It distracted her from her quiet island of pleasure. Better to find the darkness, and so she hurried to her seat where she could enjoy her freedom in quiet.

"I didn't set this up," whispered Tammy from the table. "I swear! But you were great!"

Nicky didn't respond. She simply closed her eyes and breathed in. There was no restriction here—oxygen flowed in and out without restraint. She was never, ever going to leave this island he'd created.

"Aw, don't sulk, Nicky. It was funny. In fact, it was great to see you let go like that. You need to do that more often."

Nicky nodded. She would do that. After all, he had told her exactly what to do. She was going to see him tonight at his home.

"Nicky?" *His* voice interrupted her thoughts. But of

course, he couldn't interrupt anything. He was everything! "Nicky?"

She turned, smiling warmly as she looked into his sweet mocha eyes.

"I brought you back your cell phone. No hard feelings, right?"

"Of course not," she said as she took her phone then started pulling up the Internet phone pages. There he was, Magic Man, complete with his phone number and home address.

"Nicky, you remember me, right? You remember who I am?"

She looked up just as the house lights dimmed for the next act. It didn't matter. She knew the shape and color of his eyes, just as she knew the feel of his mouth on hers. He was her island god, and she was never leaving him.

"Nicky?"

"You're the Magic Man," she answered.

His expression faltered, and even without the full lights, she could see his face twist into a self-mocking grimace. "Of course. That's exactly who I am," he said as he straightened and looked toward the bar. "And I wanted to make your every fantasy come true." That last was muttered beneath his breath, but she heard it. On this wonderful island, she was completely tuned in to his every whisper. After all, he said she'd feel safe as long as she could hear his voice.

She reached for him, but he was already moving away. She sighed. She wanted her every fantasy to come true, too. Fortunately, she had an answer. She delved into her purse for her car keys. She would go to his home. They could begin tonight.

3

JAMES RAY, AKA MAGIC MAN, didn't feel so magical as he pushed open the passenger car door. He shouldn't have drunk so much after the show. He shouldn't have done a lot of things, but seeing Nicky again had hit him like a freight train. He couldn't believe she was right there, just sitting in the audience like anybody else.

The real blow had come when he'd realized she didn't remember him. He'd even brought her up on the stage, gave her the hint about her prom night, and nothing. Not the slightest flicker of recognition in those liquid brown eyes. And her face wasn't quite the elfin pixie he remembered. She'd matured and looked more sophisticated than in high school. But still, how could she not remember him? While he, on the other hand, had picked her out of the crowd despite the glare of the footlights.

"You okay there, dude?"

He glanced back at Rick, his brother and the club owner. The man had taken one look at Jim's flushed face and demanded his car keys. Now, an hour later, they were right outside his suburban house and Jim was about to manage the Herculean feat of walking up his own driveway all by himself. He gave his brother a thumbs-up. "Yuppers, duuuude." Then he pulled out his house keys and jingled them. "I'm set. Thanks." He stepped out of the car, feeling better as the cool night air hit him in the face.

"So she didn't remember you," his brother said from inside the car. "That doesn't mean you can't get to know her again. It's not a big deal. You weren't that memorable back in high school."

"Thanks a lot," Jim muttered as he found his physical balance. His mental balance was still way off. The reality that he wasn't even a blip on Nicky's memory radar still had him reeling. Enough so that rather than pursue the woman, he'd dived face-first into a bottle of vodka.

Rick flashed him a smirk. "Plenty of fish in the sea, Jimmy. Don't forget that. Plenty of fish…" His voice faded out as he pulled away from the curb.

"In the sea," Jim returned, his buzz fading. He didn't want a fish, he wanted Nicky. Nicky who was all woman. Who had long legs beneath her boring gray skirt. Who had once put strawberry gloss on her lips right before he kissed her. Nearly ten years later, he could still taste that gloss. And she didn't even remember him.

"Don't want a fish," he muttered as he turned toward his house. It was almost too dark to see. He should have remembered to leave on the outside light. Fortunately, there was enough moonlight to see around the short, blocky hedges that edged his walkway. He'd only gone two steps when he stopped. He saw something there. A dark figure on his front steps. White flesh, dark clothing and a face tilted down into shadows. He rubbed his eyes. What he was seeing couldn't possibly be there. But when he pulled his hands away from his eyes, there she was.

He shuffled forward to see better. And miracle of miracles, she lifted her head.

"Nicky?" he rasped. It couldn't be.

She smiled at him. God, she was beautiful. "I looked you up in the yellow pages," she said. "Magic Man."

"That's me," he returned, then winced at the really lame banter. He wanted to be witty, to impress Nicky, but then he'd never managed suave around her. The best he could manage right then was to walk up to the front step.

She slowly stood to meet him, her legs slipping beneath her, her black pumps making a soft click on the stone. And as she rose, he could see something else, something that made his eyes bulge.

Her blouse was undone. Her white silk blouse was open all the way down. It simply lay against her breasts, flapping loosely. He could even see the lace cups of her bra.

"You said you wanted to make my fantasies come true," she said. "I have a fantasy." She put her hands to the bra's front clasp and popped it open. "I've dreamed of a man spending forever kissing my nipples until I come just from his mouth alone."

Then right there—outside on his front steps—she pulled her bra apart. Her breasts fell forward, milky white in the moonlight except for the dark points of her nipples. They were full and heavy right there in front of him. Perfectly shaped—a bit more than a handful—and puckered such that he thought they were pointing to him.

"I've dreamed of it forever," she said. "And you're my island god. You can—"

"I can do that," he rasped, unable to lift his eyes from her breasts.

"Would you?" she asked, and then she shrugged out of her blouse as if she meant him to do it right there on his porch!

"Inside!" he said. He grabbed her arm and managed to pull her up to his door. There was more fumbling as he tried to fit the key into his lock. And why the hell had he decided to get drunk tonight of all nights?

He shoved open the door and pulled her inside, kicking her purse in with one foot. She had stripped out of her blouse and dropped it on the railing outside. He stared at it with a frown. Something was definitely not right here. But when he turned around, he saw her pull off her bra and drop it on the floor. White lace lying on dark brown carpet.

"Nicky…" he began, doing his best to make his brain work. "Is this really your fantasy?"

"Oh, yes," she answered as she lifted her breasts in her own hands. "Your mouth on my nipples." Then she flicked herself with her thumbs, her eyes drifting shut in delight.

He couldn't have stopped if his life depended on it. He had to touch her breasts. She was offering them to him, holding them out. He had to touch. But before he could connect with her flesh, his mind made one last valiant attempt at reason. He jerked his eyes up to her face, searching her eyes for the truth.

"Do you remember me, Nicky?"

"Yes," she answered. "Of course I do."

"Have you wanted this as long as I have?"

She smiled and arched her back, simultaneously lifting her chest closer to him. "Forever."

It was all his brain needed to surrender. Nicky, his

high school dream girl, was finally here offering him her breasts. No way in hell was he going to say no to that! His gaze was back on her chest, but her hands were in the way.

"Let go," he instructed. He didn't want anything between himself and those luscious mounds.

She let her arms drop to her sides.

He reached out, his tan fingers a dark contrast to her nearly luminescent flesh. He paused. "Do you want to go to my bedroom?"

She arched her back, lifting her hands above her head. "In my fantasy, I am stretched tall."

"Standing?"

"Yes."

Good thing he had a two-story. He walked her backward to the side of his staircase. Then he took her hands and wrapped her fingers around the posts. She obeyed without resistance, and her soft pants told him she was as excited as he.

"Don't let go," he said as his gaze slid down her long arms, past her wet lips, down to the lifted expanse of her breasts. At last! He took her breasts in his hands and began to play.

NICKY CLOSED HER EYES and smiled into the darkness. At last she would feel his hands like hot oil on her skin. Finally, she would know his mouth on her breasts. She remembered intensity, she recalled gentle, tentative caresses, but she had no idea from where that memory came. She only knew it was true. It was him. And now she could feel more.

Somewhere off in the distance, she felt a nagging shock, an overwhelming pressure just waiting to crush her. But she didn't have to be crushed if she didn't want to be. She could stay right here on her island of pleasure. She was safe here because her island god decreed it so, and the ugly weight would never strike.

Besides, he was here with her now. And he was tonguing her breasts just as she'd fantasized so long ago. She didn't need to remember when. She just needed to be here, now, with him.

He began as men always do—too fast and too hard. Odd, but she found she liked it. He lifted her breasts in both hands, squeezing them just short of pain before rolling his hands forward to tweak her nipples. Since her arms were stretched over her head, her breasts were thrust forward to give him total access, total control. She couldn't even move backward away from him, which meant he could do whatever he wanted to her breasts, and she had absolutely no say in the matter.

She took a deep breath, feeling her lungs expand. His hands moved with her as he kneaded her flesh. He had gentled his touch now, so there wasn't even the threat of pain until he abruptly bit her nipple. She gasped in surprise, but her legs trembled in delight.

"Is this part of your fantasy?" he asked.

"Yes," she answered without thought, because he was right. This was exactly what she wanted. "Both breasts," she said. "Whatever and however until I come." It had been a part of her fantasy landscape since she first began dreaming of men.

He narrowed his hands until he had hold of just her nipples, tugging them both. Then he put his mouth to one breast and sucked her in, rolling her nipple around and around with his tongue. She squirmed but couldn't go far with her hands gripping the posts.

He released one nipple to work on the other. The

abandoned one felt cold and wet, but soon she felt his fingers on it, rubbing the liquid in and twisting the nub. Meanwhile, his mouth went to work on the right breast, nibbling the skin around and underneath her nipple. Her breast felt full and achy, but his every abrasion heated a fire in her belly. Her knees went weak, and her legs separated of their own accord.

Part of her wanted to stop this madness. Part of her thought her behavior was very odd, but she squelched it. Those thoughts belonged to the part of her that stumbled under the weight of her world. She would not go there. She would not think those things. She would not even acknowledge the oppressive burden that waited just at the edge of her consciousness.

Sweaty pleasure was all she wanted. He was sucking her breast rhythmically now, tonguing her nipple as he worked. Heat built from inside her belly. It rushed like a wave outward, like flash fire on her skin. Her hands tightened on the railing as she gasped in reaction. Not an orgasm, but thrilling nonetheless.

She moaned and thrust her belly against his groin. He was thick and hard, a hot brand even through his clothes. Why was he wearing clothes? She wanted to lift her skirt and wrap her legs around him—naked him—but she couldn't manage it without letting go of the posts. So she just stood there and whimpered.

He must have heard the sound because he pulled back. His hair was mussed, his mouth wet, but it was his eyes that she saw the most. Dark brown like molten gold mixed with chocolate. In this place, the analogy made sense and she willingly submerged herself in his power.

"Do you want more?" he rasped.

"Yes," she answered.

He grinned, but didn't speak. Without moving his eyes, he reached down and pulled her narrow skirt up to her waist.

Finally! She spread her legs to ease the heat. It didn't help, especially as his hands roved over her thighs.

"Thigh-high panty hose," he murmured. Then his hands stroked higher. "And a thong!" He smiled at her even as he hooked his thumbs under the strings and pushed them down. Then his grin widened as he bent his knees, kissing his way down her chest and belly.

He had to stop where her skirt was bunched at her stomach. His mouth left her skin with a swirling tongue motion that could only be described as a flourish. Then he glanced up at her.

"I'm going take this off," he said as he tugged at her thong. "But the thigh-highs stay on." Then he glanced down. "And those heels. Love the heels. They're so very corporate."

He peeled the thong down and she felt the slow pull as the wet fabric separated from her skin. He used his fingers to maneuver the strings, but his thumbs slid in and around her mound. Then he groaned in delight.

"God, Nicky, you are a fantasy come true!"

She didn't respond. She couldn't. He was looking at her again, and she was lost in the swirling colors of his eyes. Or at least her mind was; the rest of her was absorbed in the sensation of her thong dropping down past her knees to be caught around her ankles.

She wanted to reach down and unhook it from the straps of her black pumps, but her hands would not release. He had told her not to let go, so she didn't. She couldn't, not without switching her brain on, and that was something she never intended to do again. Then he relieved her discomfort by lifting her left knee.

The fabric stretched. His fingers caressed her calf and popped the cotton off. He returned her leg to the ground and shifted to her right knee. He lifted it up and she felt the thong hang in the air. She tried maneuvering her foot to shake it loose, but it was caught. How impossible that she couldn't even release the stupid thong. But then her thoughts were distracted as he kept raising her knee up. Higher and higher as he fell to the ground before her.

She stared mutely at him as he guided her knee to his shoulder, his hand still stroking the silk of her thigh-highs with a kind of reverence.

"God, I love this," he murmured against the fine hose. Then he leaned down, nipping through the silk as he roved higher on her thigh. Soon he was at the edge, murmuring something she couldn't hear against her skin.

The moment his lips touched her unprotected flesh, another flash fire of heat erupted. A split-second burst of sensation that made her hiss. He started to pull back but she didn't want that, so she tightened her leg and kept him right where he was. She even lifted her other leg and dropped it on his shoulder.

He helped her, his hands bracing on the wall behind her so that she rested on his forearms. She hung there, her core open to the cold air, her moisture making her feel wet and exposed. If she'd had the use of her hands, she would have stopped him. It was too much for her, too vulnerable.

But he had said she couldn't let go and so she tightened her thighs. The idea was to ease some of the weight off her arms, but it ended up bringing his mouth right to her center. This wasn't part of her fantasy, but it was fabulous nonetheless. Besides, she wasn't in control here. He was, and she trusted him absolutely. In this place, he was the god who made everything safe and wonderful.

Then he began to lick. Long, thick strokes. Narrow pointy thrusts. Swirling combinations of both. Another flash fire hit with his first stroke. Then came another as he flattened his tongue and pushed against her clit. Another swirl and a shudder hit her spine. Her chest lifted as a wave of volcanic heat rolled over her belly, creating a pocket of fire under her skin.

She was gasping, her back undulating against the wall. Her arms were beginning to ache, her fingers slick on the posts, but she didn't let go. The pain in her palms was nothing compared to the wonderful wet slide of his tongue.

She wanted to move her hips, to push her groin deeper and harder against his mouth. But her hands had no strength left in them. All of her weight rested on his arms and mouth. She couldn't do anything. Her only participation was to experience, and that was more than enough.

He fluttered his tongue against her clit. A rapid flip-flip-flip that pushed her violently over the edge into orgasm. The volcanic fire from before was nothing compared to this. A supernova exploded across her skin. She screamed. She bucked. She lost herself to absolute pleasure.

Ahhhh!

She tried to stay there. She tried to hold on, but eventually the nova burst faded, leaving behind a warm glow. Her hands gave out and she sank bonelessly to the floor. He went with her, still holding her as she lay there dazed and happy. She felt him shift her around so that her head pillowed against his chest, and his arms cradled her sideways against his body.

She meant to open her eyes. She meant to say something. After all, she had broken the rules by releasing hold of the railing. But there was a second fantasy, more compelling right now. It was the dream of falling asleep in his arms.

She tucked her head tight to his chest, inhaled deeply of his rich male scent and succumbed to this other fantasy.

She slept.

JIM LOOKED DOWN at the sleeping woman, surprised that he didn't feel more frustration. He could still smell her with every breath, and her taste lingered on his tongue. He was harder than a rock and could barely think for the need to bury himself to the hilt inside her.

And yet, he was holding her as she slept. This close, he could see the lines of fatigue in her face, the dark smudges beneath her eyes, only partially covered by her long eyelashes. The girl of his adolescent fantasies was asleep in his arms. The thought warmed his heart.

He settled her more deeply in his embrace, then stood up. He staggered, more from drunkenness than her weight. It wasn't easy climbing the stairs. If he hadn't spent a ridiculous number of evenings at the gym, he never would have managed it.

Fortunately, she didn't notice their near-tumbles but slept on, completely undisturbed. He made it into the bedroom and settled her on his pillow. She made the shift easily enough, sighing deeply as he pulled the sheet over her. There wasn't anything he could do about her skirt, which was twisted awkwardly beneath her, but at least she'd lost her shoes somewhere along the way.

Looking down at her, he rubbed a hand blearily over

his face. He was still hard, his erection stretching for her even now. But hot as he was for her, he couldn't stomach waking her. So he did the next best thing. He stripped and readied for bed. Then he climbed in behind her and wormed his arm beneath her shoulders before spooning her tight against him.

In one way, it was absolute torture. Here she was, with her sweet behind pressed against his swollen cock. It wouldn't take much to do what he wanted.

On the other hand, this was his own dream come true. Nicky, his high school fantasy, was asleep in his bed. There was a mint scent to her hair and the hot reminder of her still in his mind. He closed his eyes and let himself drift into his own fantasies.

Sometime later he, too, slept.

4

NICKY SMILED IN HER SLEEP. She knew she was sleeping because nowhere else felt so wonderful except, of course, that fabulous island paradise. Wait… Island paradise and the god who created it. Oh yes, the god. She shifted her legs restlessly. She liked her island god.

There was something important for her to remember about that. About him. Perhaps she should get up and look for him. Was she still on her island? She felt warm enough to be, but in this fuzzy half-awake state, she couldn't remember. Didn't really want to know. She drifted back to sleep.

She had to pee. Mentally, she sighed. She would open her eyes—just a crack—and find the bathroom. After that, she could go back to bed and keep dreaming. Reluctantly, she blinked her eyes open. She frowned. She didn't see anything familiar. That wasn't her bedside table. This wasn't her room. It didn't even smell like her house!

She tried to hold on to her blissful state. But reality became too insistent. Panic clutched her chest and pressure built. Awareness burst painful and heavy across her consciousness, and she crumpled beneath the weight. What had she done?

What had she done?

"OH, NO. OH, NO."

Jim's eyes popped open at the odd sound of a woman having hysterics in his bed. Light stabbed his eyeballs, and he immediately slammed them shut again, but the woman would not be quiet.

"Oh, no."

Memory returned with a rush. Nicky in the audience. Nicky in his hallway. Nicky on his mouth and tongue. He would have smiled if she weren't at that very moment jostling the mattress as she scrambled out of bed. He did manage to moan as the sudden cold air hit his body.

"Oh. Oh!"

This was not the morning he had envisioned last night. He cracked an eye. "Nicky?"

A door slammed nearby and the sound jolted him completely—miserably—awake. He clutched his head. How much had he drunk? It didn't matter. All that mattered now was that Nicky was obviously panicking in his bathroom.

"Nicky," he tried again, wincing at the sound. "It's okay. I know this is weird, but really, it's okay."

The only response he got was the sound of a flushing toilet. It was a really loud sound, and he clenched his shoulders as if that could hold back the pounding in his head. He thought longingly of the medicine cabinet inside his bathroom, but kept the bulk of his attention on listening for Nicky. She was running the sink tap now. Why wouldn't she speak to him?

"Come on, Nicky." He tried again as he pushed to his

feet and stumbled over to the dresser. Fumbling around, he managed to find a pair of sweats and pull them on. "We've known each other forever. This doesn't have to be weird."

It was a lie, of course. Being neighborhood pals back when they were twelve made everything more surreal, not less. Especially since they hadn't really been pals. More like, oh-there's-that-kid-who-lives-down-the-street acquaintances. And yet, because of that wonderful prom night, she was so much more important to him than just that. He scrubbed a hand over his face and went to lean against the bathroom door. "You have to come out of there sometime, you know."

It took a few moments more before he heard the tap shut off. And then a soft voice wavered through the door. "Um…do you…um…know where my clothes are?"

Okay, that did not sound good. Her voice was high and tight, but he tapped down his nervousness and made sure his voice sounded calm. Stay casual, he told himself. It's no big deal. And wasn't that the lie of the century?

"Sure. I'll go grab them." He made quick work of it, though it took him a moment to find her blouse on his porch railing. Even with his hangover, he couldn't resist smiling at that, not to mention what they'd done at his staircase railing. Last night had been beyond anything he could have expected. Now he just had to make sure she stayed in his life.

"I've got your clothes," he said when he returned to his bedroom. "Did you want—"

The door opened a crack and a hand snaked out to grab her clothes. He tried to delay a bit. He didn't hold on to the clothes, but he put his other hand on the door and tried to talk calmly.

"You want coffee or something? I've got…um…bagels. And cereal."

It didn't work. He caught the briefest glimpse of big eyes and dark circles. Lower down, his blue towel wrapped around pale skin. Then the door was firmly shut again.

He sighed. His head was pounding too much for him to think clearly. He wanted to be suave, to say something that would make it all better for her, but he just didn't know what that would be. And while he was still standing there without a clue, the door to the bathroom quietly opened.

He tried a winning smile. "Hey there."

She looked pale standing there in her wrinkled business suit. Her hair was loose, falling about her face in pretty waves. But it was the bruised look to her eyes that held his attention. And that she wouldn't look him in the face.

"Nicky…" he began, but stopped when she flinched.

"No, thanks," she said, her voice cracking slightly. "About the coffee. But if you… Do you know where my shoes are?"

He blinked and looked down at her bare feet. Her feet were unadorned. Even her toenails weren't painted, and he found the sight oddly delightful. If only she didn't look as if she was about to bolt.

"You kicked them off downstairs, I think." He didn't say what they'd been doing when she lost them. But then he saw the hot flash of color in her cheeks, and he knew her mind had already gone there.

He shifted awkwardly, wishing he knew what to do. "Let me take you out to breakfast. We can talk. Catch up."

She shook her head. At least that's what he thought she did, though it was hard to tell, given the tight set to her shoulders. "Um, I have to get to work."

"I really want to talk to you, Nicky. Just talk."

She bit her lip and he realized that, except for that small movement, she appeared to be frozen in place. When she spoke, her words came out in a high whisper. "Look, you don't know this about me, but last night... I never... I mean, that's not me. I don't...do that." Her eyes darted briefly for a moment to his bed, then back to the floor.

He looked at her, and his mind struggled with her words. If he weren't so hungover, maybe he'd be quicker on the uptake. "Of course I know that. Nicky..." He took a step forward, and she gave a little pip of a squeak and shied backward. She was scared of him! He stared at her, his mind fumbling through the facts.

"What's my name, Nicky?"

She didn't answer. At best, her eyes went wider in horror.

He swallowed, feeling the sucker punch to his gut once again. It shouldn't make a difference. So she didn't remember who he was. His brother was right: he hadn't been that memorable in high school. But this was Nicky. He'd shared the best night of his life with her. He'd forged a connection with her, damn it. Twice! Back years ago on prom night and again last night. She had to remember him.

"What's my name, Nicky?" He still spoke quietly, but the gentle had gone out of him. His words came out more as a low command.

"Magic?" she finally said.

He stared at her, his pounding headache receding beneath the bare truth. "No," he said slowly. "That's not my name. Nicky, look at me." He was pleading now, praying that in the harsh light of day she could look at him and know him. In fact, he stepped over to the curtains, hauling them open so that the sun shone harsh on his features.

She winced at the sudden flare of light. He did, too, for that matter. She swallowed and visibly drew in a breath, obviously trying to steady herself. Lord, he hated seeing her like that. She looked as if she was about to throw up.

"Let me give you a hint. We went to high school together."

She blinked. Her expression shifted away from nausea, more to an intense confusion as she peered at him.

With a curse of disgust, he grabbed his glasses from his dresser and plopped them on his nose. "How about now?" he asked, then he gazed at her with a moony-eyed adoration that was, unfortunately, reflected in the mirror. He only saw it in his peripheral vision, but it was enough to churn up a well of self-disgust.

"Oh, my god! Jimmy Ray?"

"I go by Jim now. Sometimes James."

Her hands dropped to her sides as she frowned, looking at him from top to bottom and then back up again. Her shoulders relaxed, but only a fraction of an inch. And then she just shook her head. "Jimmy," she murmured, half to herself. "You've filled out."

"I work out," he returned. And was there ever a more inane conversation?

"Wow, Jimmy…uh, Jim." She bit her lip. "You're…a magician?"

He shook his head. "I'm an engineer who plays a magician on amateur night. Rick—my brother—owns the club and he calls me when they're short an act." Then his pride forced him to add, "But I'm a good engineer, so I've done well. And I'm taking a little time off right now. To...um...play."

"Ah," she said, nodding her head. He could tell she didn't know what to say any more than he did. "Well, you always were good at anything you tried."

Not true. He'd tried to impress her and had obviously failed miserably. But saying that would be surly. Humiliating, too. "You look like you're doing well," he said, gesturing to her wrinkled clothing. "Power suit and all."

"Corporate America and all its pressures." She shrugged. "I manage some distribution nodes for Korner Plastics."

"Impressive."

"Not really. It just requires a lot of time and attention to detail."

"And you always sold yourself short," he returned.

She didn't answer. There was something in her eyes that he remembered, a vulnerability or an ache maybe. As if she wanted to believe what he said, but was too afraid. He shifted uncomfortably on his feet, the déjà vu making him reel. Hadn't they played this scene before? Like ten years ago on prom night?

Before he could answer that question, a double electronic note sounded from downstairs. Beepbeep. Beepbeep. Her eyes widened, and her gaze hopped to the red numbers on his clock—9:14.

"Oh, crap. Crapcrapcrapcrapcrap!" Then she dashed downstairs.

He followed more slowly, mostly because he didn't know what to say to her. He knew she was seconds away from rushing out the door, but for the life of him, he couldn't figure out how he felt about that. This whole situation was just too bizarre.

By the time he made it to the first floor, she'd located her phone and was paging through messages. At least she'd stopped cursing, though he could hardly call it an improvement. Now her lips were pursed tight and her back was visibly hunched over her phone.

"Nicky..." he began. "I really want to talk to you..." He let his voice trail away. She wasn't even looking at him but down at her phone. He'd faded from her conscious mind, her attention fixed on more important matters. Boy, did he remember this feeling. Ignored. Unimportant. How many times had he stood in the background watching her as she did something with someone else?

Well, he wasn't that pathetic high school kid anymore. He wasn't the school nerd with braces and acne. And he damn well was a decade beyond mooning after the hot volleyball player. With a snort of disgust, he turned his back on her and went into his bathroom. So maybe it was peevish of him to slam the door, but the resounding bang felt good.

This time he liked his reflection in the mirror. He looked strong and adult. All traces of adolescent yearning were erased from his body. Then he heard the front door open and close, and he sighed, accepting the truth. He'd had his shot at Nicky, and he'd failed. But that was it for him. A man could only take so much humiliation.

"Goodbye, Nicky."

5

"LET'S GO OUT again tonight."

Thanks to the miracles of Bluetooth, Nicky didn't even need to take her hands off her keyboard to answer her little sister. "Sorry, Tammy, I've got to—"

"Work. No, you don't. It's Friday."

Nicky didn't even bother trying to explain that this crisis was different. Her boss had made it clear that if she even whispered the word layoff, she'd be fired on the spot. So she didn't say anything. But it was one more stresser which threatened to send her over the edge. She keyed a new number into her spreadsheet and studied the result.

"Nicky!"

"Hmm? Oh, sorry. I can't. I got in late today, this report isn't setting up right, and—"

"And it's Friday! Come on, Nicky. You had a good time last night, didn't you?"

Her fingers froze over the number pad and her heart started thudding triple time. Her sister had finally managed to grab all her attention. "What do you mean?"

"What do you mean, what do I mean?"

Nicky clenched the edge of her desk, forcing herself to keep her voice normal. Even. "Tammy, I am not in the mood to play."

"Like that's different. Come on, sis, you relaxed last night. You were almost serene there at the end, don't you remember? You actually forgot your phone on the table. I had to grab you and drop it into your purse. When was the last time that happened? You forgetting your cell?"

"Never," Nicky murmured. Then she shook her head, though no one was there to see her. She didn't remember forgetting her phone. She just remembered her sunlit island paradise and the god who'd created it for her. That the "god" was actually Jimmy Ray from high school just added more confusion to the whole situation. He'd been a friend when she needed one. A sweet guy she'd liked but never really thought much about in high school. Her life was too busy with other things, with flashier things, if she were to be honest.

But Jimmy Ray wasn't forgettable now. She should know. She'd been trying to forget him all day, only to catch herself a moment later remembering the feel of his hands on her, the stroke of his tongue—and the way she had felt so absolutely free with him. That was the part she really couldn't forget. She'd felt so safe that she had let herself do whatever sprang into her head with him. That hadn't happened to her before. Ever.

What would she give to go to that place again? The question had been tantalizing her all day long. But then reality would hit with a gut-twisting wrench. She had school loans to pay off, a condo the bank mostly owned, a nest egg that was more like a nest prayer. She had to work, damn it. Jobs were on the line, and not just hers. So she swiveled her office chair to page through the dozens of papers on her desk, but her mind wasn't really on her task. It had wandered somewhere else completely. "Hey, do you remember Jim from high school?"

There was a long pause on the other end of the line. "Jim who?"

"Jimmy. Dorky Jimmy—"

"Math geek guy! Yeah, his brother, Rick, owns the club we went to last night. What ever happened to him?"

"He became the Magic Man and starred on amateur night."

"No way!" Tammy's voice echoed the same shock that still reverberated through Nicky's brain. "Can't be. The Magic Man was...well, he was..."

"Cute. I know."

"Hot. I bet he has killer pecs under that tux."

Oh, yes. Jimmy Ray did indeed have killer pecs. She'd gotten an up close look at them this morning.

"Oh, wow. I never would have guessed that. How'd you find out?"

"Um...it just came to me this morning." Right after she'd woken up spooned against him.

"Oh," Tammy said, obviously disappointed. "Then you don't *know,* you're just guessing. Which means it's not him."

"Trust me," Nicky drawled, "it's him."

"Trust you on a people thing. Hmmm. Nope, don't think so."

Nicky frowned and she actually lifted her gaze from the reports on her desk. "No really. It's him."

"No really, sis, you suck at people memory. Numbers, shipping lanes, even employees—not a problem. But real people? Not so much."

"That doesn't even make sense!"

"What doesn't make sense is that you're a gorgeous

woman who spends all her time working. What's up with that, Nicky? Get out of the office! Practice those rusty people skills. Come to the comedy club with me tonight."

Nicky sighed. They'd come full circle in this conversation. Unfortunately, she couldn't bring herself to agree with her sister. Not after last night's disastrous escapade. At the moment, she just wanted to slink her way home, bury her head under the pillows and not come out until next year.

"Sorry, Tammy," she finally said, her breath short because of the tightness in her chest. "I really do have a lot of work to do. Maybe tomorrow. Or next week. That'd be better."

"Yeah, sure. Like that'll happen," her sister groused.

"Don't be like that—" Nicky began, but Tammy interrupted.

"You're going to have to face life someday, Nicky. One day you're going to look up and realize you've spent yours trapped in that hole you call an office."

"Tammy—"

"Gotta go. It's time for my pedicure. Bye!"

The line went dead. Nicky grimaced as she pulled the earpiece off her head. Then she stared at the Bluetooth connector. Did it mean something that her ear felt weird without the thing attached to her head?

She looked down at the reports on her desk, flicking her eyes at her computer screen. There was a ton of work for her to do here, but she couldn't force herself back to it. Her mind kept wandering.

It had been that way all day. As much as she tried to lose herself in her job, certain memories kept intruding. There wasn't any particular order to the thoughts. She'd flash on Jimmy standing naked and angry before her. Then Jimmy onstage as the Magic Man. Then Jimmy's hurt expression when he realized she hadn't a clue who he was. And most jarring of all, the loud bang of his bathroom door this morning when she wouldn't even talk to him.

It wasn't that her morning e-mails had been all that important or that she'd needed to absolutely read every last one that second. But what did she say to the man who had rocked her world the night before? Nerdy Jimmy Ray had given her the best orgasm of her life, and she just didn't know what to say about that. She didn't even know what to think about that, except that she wanted more.

She'd never had a one-night stand before. Never really had time, to tell the truth. So rather than face him this morning, she'd buried her nose in her phone and pretended not to be excruciatingly aware of his amazing half-naked body less than three feet away from her. Then he'd stomped away in disgust—not that she blamed him—and she'd boogied out the door as fast as she could move in three-inch pumps.

Now here she was at the end of an unproductive work day, and she still couldn't get him out of her mind. He'd hypnotized her, seriously put her deep in a way she never thought possible. So much so that she'd gone to his house and told him about her nipple fantasy. How had he done that?

Her face heated to crimson at just the thought. At least she hadn't confessed any of her *other* fantasies. Nipples were the most mundane of what she wanted. But still, whatever would possess her to tell him that? To stalk him at night to do that?

She leaned back in her chair in stunned shock. The

answer was obvious. She *wouldn't* do that. Ever. Stalk a stranger and tell him her fantasies? *Never.*

Which meant someone else had made her do it. Jimmy. He had put in a posthypnotic suggestion or something. He'd planted something in her brain so powerful that she had leaped right over all her inhibitions and gone straight to hot sex in his house. Good God, it wasn't possible! And yet…she had no other explanation for her behavior.

She snatched up her phone and quickly found his number. Then she started to thumb it in, only stopping herself with a physical jerk.

What was she doing? If he had truly planted some powerful suggestion in her brain, then she ought to be running screaming in the other direction. She stared at the number on her phone. The compulsion to hit Send was so strong! She wanted…no, she needed to talk to him, to see him again. Why? What for? For an embarrassing repeat of this morning? Never! So why the need to call him?

Was she still hypnotized? Still under the grip of his mental suggestion or something? Everything inside her rebelled at the thought. She was a smart, intelligent woman. She couldn't possibly be under some hypnotic influence. Maybe she'd just really, really needed to get off, so to speak. That was way more logical than some heebie-jeebie hypnosis. But then why waste hours today thinking about him? This report was the most important thing in her life right now. Close to a thousand jobs were at stake. She needed to get it done and get it done right! She had to put all thoughts of Jimmy away.

With sudden resolve, she put down her phone. She was going to focus exclusively on work for the next couple hours. But just as she made to turn the thing off, her breath started to choke in her throat. With a dispassionate stare, she saw that her palms were slick with sweat. Next came the pain between her shoulder blades that expanded through her chest along with the spikes that split through her temples.

Another panic attack. They'd started about a year ago. Nothing major. They'd only happened a couple times before. She always hyperventilated in a sweaty, can't breathe, can't live kind of way, but then it faded. She just had to wait it out. She'd learned to distance her mind from the disaster that was going on through her body. She wasn't going to die. She wasn't going to stop breathing. She just had to live through the agony shooting through her chest. It would pass. It would pass, would pass…pass…

She sat sprawled in her office chair. Her blouse was plastered to her sweating torso and she was still panting. But the pain was receding, she was indeed taking in real oxygen, and she had not died. The panic attack was gone, and she would soon feel normal once again.

She glanced up at her office door. It was still closed. No one had come in, no one knew what had happened, so she could pretend it never had. That was, in truth, the reason why she had taken to closing her office door. These attacks were much more disturbing to other people than they were to her. They passed. The pain receded. She could go back to her real life now.

The real question was why it had happened just then. The answer, of course, was right there on her desk. The attack had hit at the very idea that she *not* contact Jimmy. Something was going on here. Something more than fantasy island sex.

She grimaced as she lifted her hair off her neck. The brush of air across her sweaty skin felt nice, but it also solidified her resolve. This had to end, whatever *this* was. Her life was difficult enough without having sex fests push her into sweaty panic attacks. She snatched up her phone and hit the send button.

6

THIS WAS A BAD IDEA, Jim thought as he crossed the street and headed down the block. This was perhaps one of the worst ideas he'd ever had. But when Nicky had called him, clearly overwrought, he hadn't been able to say no. She'd spouted all sorts of nonsense, something about him putting a posthypnotic sex idea in her head. She hadn't sounded angry, really. More distraught in a way that went beyond one-night-stand embarrassment. And that's what did him in. He couldn't ever resist a damsel in distress, especially when that damsel was Nicky.

It wasn't PC of him, was certainly not something he'd confess to anyone in this day and age. But yeah, he had a chivalrous streak a mile wide. When a woman was in trouble, he couldn't resist running to her rescue any way he could. And since this particular woman was Nicky, he was doomed the moment he'd picked up the phone. So here he was, about to enter a café near his home, just because he couldn't stop the stupid swell in his chest that made him want to be Nicky's magic man.

He pulled upon the restaurant's door with a fatalistic

shrug. Only about half the tables were full, so he saw her immediately. Hard to miss her tight bun, dark suit and legs that went up to her neck. Everything about her was neat, precise and so hot he nearly broke out in a sweat.

She liked a lace bra beneath that demure silk blouse. He knew what she smelled like when her thong was dripping wet. And he knew the sounds of abandon she made when she came apart on his lips. He'd peeled back the layers of her tight, corporate exterior and touched the wanton beneath. And damn if he didn't want to do it again.

The restaurant was narrow, the tables marching in a straight line back from the front door. There were more intimate booths along the side, but she'd chosen a table dead center in the room. He took his time crossing to her, studying her as he moved. She'd set her menu to the side and was sitting precisely still. The only sign of agitation came from the way she kept crossing and uncrossing her legs beneath the table. She linked her feet together at the ankle, then released them to push one heeled pump into the floor. Then she flattened her foot before crossing her ankles again. He counted five shifts in the time it took him to make it to her side.

"Hello, Nicky. You look very corporate tonight."

Her gaze shot to him, and he could see that her face was still tinged with panic. Her eyes were wide, her mouth pinched, and she kept her jaw tightly clenched.

"I—I don't know how to answer that," she said. "Was that a compliment or a jab?"

"Just a statement of fact," he said as he slid in beside her. "Does it have to be something more?"

Her gaze followed him with a wary anxiety. "I don't

know. The Jimmy I remember didn't have any guile. I don't know about the Magic Man."

He almost laughed at that. He'd picked that name with her in mind. Well, her and the Heart song. Either way, he'd wanted to be mesmerizingly special to a girl. To Nicky. Who was staring at him as if he was about to turn into a serial killer. He sighed.

"'Jimmy' sounds like a pet dog. My name is Jim now. I sometimes even go by James. But not Jimmy, not the Magic Man, not anything weird."

She nodded slowly, and her eyes lost some of the anxiety in them. "Okay. Jim. Thank you for coming to see me."

He didn't have a chance to respond as the waitress delivered coffee to the table for her, then asked him if he wanted a drink. He ordered a soft drink and dinner without even looking at the menu. He'd had his own share of confusion about yesterday. He'd spent a good deal of his adolescence mooning after Nicky. Last night had been a fantasy come true for him, but this morning's scene had hurt. She'd meant so much to him way back when. That she didn't even remember him come morning had cut deep. Even though he wasn't an anxious kid anymore, he sure as hell didn't want to expose himself to more pain. But if he had a real shot at Nicky, an honest shot for a relationship, then he didn't want to throw that away.

Which left him confused and nervous and all the things he thought he'd outgrown. So rather than talk to her, he stalled with food. At least if he was eating, he wouldn't be struggling for something to say to her. Besides, they made the best meat loaf here, especially when layered with extra barbecue sauce.

When the waitress turned for Nicky's order, Ms. Corporate shook her head. "I'm not hungry," she said.

He arched a brow at her. "The brain needs food to work right. How many years have you lived on just coffee?"

She quirked a brow at him. "I eat," she said defensively. "Just not when…not…" Her face tightened into a grimace. "My stomach isn't so settled right now."

"How about a bowl of soup? If memory serves, your favorite was broccoli cheddar."

Her eyes widened. "You remember that?"

That and a whole lot more, but he didn't say that. Instead, he looked at the waitress. "She'll have the broccoli cheddar in a bread bowl." The waitress nodded and walked away, which left him once again sitting awkwardly across from Nicky. And one look at her face told him she was feeling at least as anxious as he was.

He shifted in his seat and decided to go straight for the honest truth. "I didn't plant a post, pre, or during hypnosis suggestion, Nicky. It was a stage act. I made you throw your cell into a volcano. And sing. You still sing beautifully, by the way. Still in the church choir?"

She shook her head. "I gave that up years ago. No time."

"Pity."

She didn't answer, choosing instead to bury her face in her coffee mug.

"I didn't ask you to come to my house, to undress on my porch, or anything else beyond that," he said.

"Yes, you did," she said, her voice tight and high.

"No, Nicky—"

"You said, 'And I wanted to make your fantasies come true.' I heard you say that and…" She bit her lip as her gaze zipped to his face then darted away again. "I heard you say that and I was still…hypnotized or something…and…and…"

He frowned, thinking back. He remembered exactly when he'd said those words, but she couldn't have heard them. The bar was so noisy. She couldn't possibly have heard him. Except she obviously had.

He leaned forward. "Even so, even if you did hear what I'd said and you were still hypnotized, that's not a compulsion. I didn't make you do anything last night. That's not how hypnotism works. I can't make you do anything you don't want to."

She looked down at her hands where she gripped her coffee mug. "I know," she finally said. "I looked it up on the Internet. But…" She shook her head. "I would never, ever do that on my own."

He looked at her. Truthfully, he believed her. The uptight executive across from him didn't look as if she would crack a smile, much less scream while her legs were wrapped around his neck. But she had. So clear, she was capable of doing things that her corporate persona did not suggest.

She shifted again in her seat, obviously feeling excruciatingly uncomfortable. "I—" She took a deep breath and lifted her gaze to look him in the eye. "I remember everything from last night. I remember…" She swallowed. "I liked being under, Jimmy. I didn't want to come out of it."

He stared at her, trying to process what she was saying. Sure, he'd heard of people doing that. Of subjects so suggestible that they stayed hypnotized. But he'd never have pegged Nicky as one of them. She was too in control for that. But then again, maybe that was exactly the point. Maybe hypnosis was the only way she could let her inner vixen out, so to speak. And once released, that part of her didn't want to be caged up again. It sounded far-fetched to him, but then so did a lot of hypnosis stories he'd read.

"Like I said, even hypnotized, Nicky, I can't make you do anything you didn't want to."

"What if it was the alcohol? Maybe I had a bad reaction to it. Maybe there was something in it that made me more susceptible or something."

He frowned, stunned by the lengths she would go to preserve her illusion of…of what? Purity? Wholesomeness? Corporate mannequin? "Why is it so hard to believe that you just wanted to have sex with me?"

She flushed and toyed with her mug. "I'm just trying to make sense of this. I don't do stuff like that. And then today…" She shook her head. "I couldn't work. I couldn't focus. I kept thinking about…stuff."

Well, that made two of them. He didn't get a damn thing done today either. But he didn't get a chance to say that. The waitress arrived with their food, breaking the flow of the conversation. They ate in silence for a moment. Nicky was delicately efficient with her soup, of course. But he caught a glimpse of the vixen underneath when she took her first sip. Her eyes closed in delight and her mouth curved on a soft smile. It was another moment before she spoke.

"This is really good soup."

He smiled, happy that he had brought her this simple pleasure. Happy, too, that she had relaxed enough to enjoy something so ordinary as good soup.

"You're right," she said. "Broccoli cheddar is my favorite."

"You're hard to forget, Nicky," he said quietly.

She looked at him, her body shifting once again

beneath the table. But her eyes remained direct as if she had come to a decision. Then she spoke, her voice almost too quiet to hear, but he caught every word.

"This afternoon. When I thought you wouldn't see me…when I planned to never see you again…" She tore off a piece of her bread bowl but didn't eat it. "I had a…a panic attack."

His gaze leaped to her face. She wasn't looking at him, but he could see the way she bit her lip, then shifted into a self-conscious grimace.

"I've never admitted that before. That I have…episodes, you know."

"Panic attacks?"

She flinched. "I call it industrial-sized heartburn."

"But they're not," he pressed. "They—"

"Yeah, I know what they are," she interrupted before he could name them again. Then her gaze rose to him. "I know why I have them. Pressure at work and all. Reports due, bad economy, yada yada. It's hard, you know. And sometimes my body, you know, reacts."

"Maybe your body, you know, is trying to tell you something," he said smoothly.

She sighed. "I know that. And like I said, I know why I have them. Except for this last one. The one because of you."

"Because you weren't going to see me again?" he asked. The very idea hit him broadside. Nicky—this gorgeous, put-together, grown-up Nicky—had had a panic attack at the fear of *not* seeing him again. His ego just loved that! But that didn't mean he was unaffected by her obvious distress. "What happened to you, Nicky? How did you go from star athlete and class president to…" How did he say this? "You weren't wound so tight in high school."

She smiled, but the expression was almost tragic. "Nothing happened, Jimmy. I just grew up. I've got school debts and a mortgage on my condo. My job is insane, but I can't afford to quit. Not in this economy, and certainly not without another job lined up." She pulled off another piece of her bread bowl but didn't eat it. "I just need to get keep my nose to the grindstone for a little bit longer. Just through this patch and then I can breathe again."

He looked at her and saw the dark smudges under her eyes, even covered by make up. Her shoulders were hunched and her breath was short. And she'd stopped eating in favor of toying with her food. She looked haunted or dogged or just plain exhausted.

"Nicky," he said softly, "whatever the problem is, it goes way beyond last night."

She shook her head, her expression defiant. "There is no problem. Not really. I just need to understand what happened so that I can go back to work."

"I don't have your answers." But God, how he wished he did.

She set down her spoon and looked at him, her heart in her eyes. "I want you to do it to me again."

He froze, his mind spasming with ideas that had no business being in his head. He'd gone from eating his meal to rock-hard and horny in less than a breath. "What?" he managed to gasp.

"Hypnotize me. Or unhypnotize me. Or whatever. Just put me under again and tell me to go back to work."

He blinked, his disappointment keen. Not that he had really expected her to want him to repeat certain other activities, but still, that didn't stop his dick from being frustrated. "Um, that's the last thing I'd tell you to do. You're exhausted, you have panic attacks and you're thinner than a runway model. Nicky, you need a vacation."

"Just humor me, Jimmy." Then she held up her hand before he could correct her. "Jim. Please. Put me under again and unsuggest—"

"That you share your fantasies with me?"

She flushed scarlet. The shift was startling. Who knew her face could get that red that fast?

"Yes," she said softly.

He huffed, torn between his honest desire to help her and the sneaky, depraved thought that once Nicky the Vixen was released, all sorts of fun things could happen. Which was case and point for why he should not be the one hypnotizing. "Wouldn't a trained professional be a better idea? I'm a stage act, but there are psychotherapists. Doctors who are trained with hypnosis."

"No!" She shook her head so sharply, a lock of hair escaped from her bun. "It has to be you."

"Why?"

"I don't know." When he tried to make eye contact, she slurped her soup while avoiding his gaze.

"This isn't a good idea," he said over his dick's loud objection.

She lifted her gaze. "It has to be you." He opened his mouth to argue, but she held up her hand. "Please don't ask me why. I don't know. Just everything in me says it has to be you."

"After everything that's happened between us, what makes you think it would work a second time? You have to trust your hypnotist. I don't think—"

"I trust you," she said. The words were rushed, but they were absolute.

"But—"

"I trust you, Jimmy. I always have."

He studied her face. For perhaps the first time today, she was absolutely still and not the statuelike, I'm-about-to-lose-it still. She was confident in what she said. In fact, looking at her now, he was forcibly reminded of the high school girl she'd once been. And maybe that was it. Maybe she needed a psychological return to prom night when he was the one who had saved her from her asshole date. Or maybe it was more complicated than that. He hadn't a clue what was going on in her beautiful head. Either way, it didn't matter. She'd come to him for help and he'd never been able to refuse her.

"Okay," he said as he forked up a mouthful of meat loaf. "But we have to do it at my place. I can't just hypnotize you here."

She didn't even flinch. "Yeah, I figured."

"And order something more to eat. Everything makes more sense when your stomach isn't in knots from hunger."

She looked up at him sharply. "That's exactly what you said to me prom night."

Had he? He didn't remember. "Well, it's still good advice." He was being gruff with her, trying to cut the tension in him with macho orders, but she didn't seem to mind. And everything he said was good sense. Still, he couldn't shake the feeling that he was stepping into something that was going to turn his life inside out. Looking up, he gestured to the waitress before turning back to Nicky. "Get a full meal including dessert. Then we'll go back to my place and...we'll see."

"You'll hypnotize me?"

He nodded. "I'll do what I can, if you still want me to."

She smiled and he saw relief in her eyes. "You're still

Jimmy, even if you call yourself Jim. I know I'm safe with you."

He didn't respond to that because she was busy ordering dinner, but in his mind he felt a real sense of panic growing. He wasn't geek Jimmy anymore, too afraid to go for what he wanted. Which meant she wasn't even remotely safe with him if she descended into sex kitten mode again.

On the other hand, he was finally getting a real shot at Nicky Taylor, one where she knew exactly who he was and wanted to spend more time with him. Sure it was twisted up with hypnotism and fantasies, but he wasn't one to question luck—good, bad or twisted. Besides, he had a few questions burning in his head, things that only an open, responsive Nicky would answer.

Which meant he was going to do it. He was going to hypnotize her, and once she was under, he was going to find out exactly what a man had to do to get Nicky in his life forever. That was the new plan. Everything would be fine just as long as he kept his libido under control.

7

NICKY FELT A TREMOR of anxiety skate down her spine as she stepped into Jimmy—er, Jim's home. She remembered waiting for him on his porch. She remembered stripping off her blouse and the way he pushed her inside. Right over there was where she flattened herself against the stair and grabbed hold of the railing. And where he...

She swallowed and forcibly turned away from the marks her shoes had made on his wall. But the only other place to look was at Jim, and he was watching her with a kind of predatory gleam that was so unlike the Jimmy in her memory.

He didn't speak, just arched a brow at her. It was a rather dashing look, really, filled with magical mystery and daring. Add to that her memory of his lean, sculpted body and her insides went liquid. Good lord, it was already starting! She was already wet from just stepping into his home.

"Maybe this isn't a good idea," she murmured.

He shrugged, though there was a tightness in the

movement. "It's completely up to you, Nicky. It always has been."

She nodded and looked at the door. She'd driven her own car here so that she could leave whenever she wanted, but she didn't move. Her legs actually trembled at the idea of leaving. She wanted to be here. She wanted to be with *him*. And that was crazy.

"I have to find out what's going on. I just need to understand."

He nodded slowly. "I swear I'll try to help however I can. You won't be under any compulsion to tell me your secret fantasies. You don't have to do anything you don't want to."

"Like climb your wall and experience a screaming orgasm on your tongue?" She'd meant to make a joke of last night, to bring the pink elephant out into the open and laugh at it. But the moment she said the words, she nearly bit off her tongue. The memories were too close to the surface, too real to make light of them. And bringing them up like that just made her want to run back to her car...or climb up the stairway railing again. "Um, sorry. I shouldn't have said that. I'm just starting to panic, you know. I don't know what I want and I don't understand—"

"Take a breath, Nicky. You're safe with me, remember?"

She did. She took a deep breath and then another. But the hunger still simmered just beneath her skin. She needed...something. "I'm staying," she said firmly. "I know you won't hurt me."

He nodded as if that's what he expected her to say. "If nothing else, we'll get some more data on exactly what's going on."

She blinked, then felt her expression soften into

a smile. "That sounded just like high school Jimmy Ray."

He grimaced as if that weren't a compliment. "I'm not Jimmy anymore, Nicky. I'm a grown man—"

"Hey!" she said, holding up her hand. "I liked Jimmy. I was young and stupid and didn't appreciate him, but that's my fault. Don't go dissing Jimmy. He was great."

He jerked slightly, his head going back as if what she'd said surprised him. She didn't know why; it was the truth. It was just weird because she wasn't used to thinking of dorky Jimmy Ray as tall, dark and ripped. She'd come here to get some answers, but she was at serious risk of getting distracted by how very sexy he'd become. She'd spent half the time at the restaurant watching his mouth and remembering those amazing things he could do with those lips, that tongue. It wasn't appropriate, given that she wanted to fix whatever was wrong with her and go back to her normal life—hell, it was rather depraved, but apparently her lust didn't care. He was a good-looking guy, and he'd given her the best orgasm of her life. She wouldn't be human if she didn't think about what more they could do together.

Maybe she could give him a call later. Maybe once the threat of layoffs were over at work, she could invite him out for a drink. They could get to know each other as people. It was a good plan, a responsible plan—and a plan that couldn't be implemented for months at least.

She grimaced. Her chest was tightening, and a sinking depression settled into the pit of her stomach. It was the same depression that came when she realized her vacation was months away. Was she ever going to catch a break? Why did the hottest guy she'd ever met have to come into her life at the absolute worst time?

"What are you thinking, Nicky? Your face has gone all tragic."

She blinked, consciously smoothing out her expression. "It's nothing. I was just thinking that I wish I'd been smarter in high school."

He snorted, but the sound was kind. "You're not the only one who has adolescent regrets. My brother tells me that I wasn't that memorable back then."

She paused, sensing an underlying issue. "That's not true, you know. I remember Jimmy Ray quite clearly. I just…well, I would never have expected him to be onstage doing a hypnotism act. And certainly not looking as…uh…" Hot. Ripped. Studly. "Good as you do now."

He arched a brow at her. "Is that a compliment, Ms. Taylor?"

"It is, Mr. Ray. Both to the boy you were and the man you've become." She ventured a tentative smile. "And I, um, I like the way you've grown up."

His expression lightened at her words, his face becoming more boyish and approachable. She felt herself start to relax, feeling safe again. In the back of her mind, she felt the silent beckoning of her tropical island paradise and the god who made it. But she also felt Jimmy, solid and dependable Jimmy Ray, right here beside her keeping her safe.

"Let's step in here," he said, gesturing into his living room. She nodded and followed as they stepped into a very tastefully decorated man's playroom. The room was dominated by a flat-screen TV, complete with TiVo and Wii. Guitar Hero lay discarded next to speakers that went to the ceiling. And most appealing of all, he had a recliner sofa, tasteful chaise lounge and matching game seats, all in a stroke-able black velvetlike material. Very soft, very guy. And with a touch on the remote control, the curtains closed, the lighting shifted to theater mode, and gothic wall sconces flickered to life with electric "fire."

She stared at the wall sconces. "Modern-day meets Dracula?"

"It was a gift from a friend. She thought my life needed some character."

Nicky noted the "she," but didn't comment. It shouldn't bother her that he had a female friend who gave him wall sconces. She had no right to be jealous, he'd only just stepped back into her life, and yet she felt a tinge of annoyance despite all logic. Her island god was supposed to be hers alone.

"It's very nice," she forced herself to say as she sat down on the sofa. God, she just sank right into the cushions. She forcibly restrained herself from stroking the fabric. "Okay. Let's do it."

He laughed. The sound was sudden and startled her into opening her eyes. He stood right before her, his arms folded across his chest. His muscles bulged beneath his tee, and his eyes seemed to flicker as they reflected the wall sconce's fake fire. "Wow, you have some bizarre ideas about hypnotism."

He grabbed an ottoman, set it directly in front of her, then plopped down on it. This close, she could see forearm muscles as they flexed. She'd always thought him kind of soft in high school, but that had obviously changed. In fact, a lot of things about him had changed, she thought as she mentally tabulated the cost of his toys. As a kid, his family had struggled financially. His dad was an electrician who drank beer, she recalled. A *lot* of beer. And his mom…well, she didn't remember his mom doing much of anything. But obviously circumstances had changed.

She'd looked him up on the Internet this morning and had been stunned by what she discovered. He was more than a good engineer. He was a *brilliant* engineer and a millionaire because of it. Add that to the changes in his physique and the fact that he could now talk about things other than *Star Trek* and calculus and…well, he was one appealing package.

He interrupted her thoughts with a touch on her knee, one that brought her attention abruptly back to him. "First thing we have to do is get you to relax."

He'd touched her skin only for a split second, but it brought her flesh to burning alertness. "That's so unlike me," she abruptly confessed.

He raised his eyebrows. "Composed, hyperaware of your surroundings, and a little skittish when nervous? You seem *exactly* like yourself to me," he said softly.

She frowned. "Is that how I seem to you? Is that how I was in high school?"

He nodded.

She shook her head. "I was on the top of the world in high school. Queen of my set, managed school and volleyball without a hitch." She almost referred to her wrestling team boyfriend, but didn't want to go there. She'd had *lousy* taste in guys in high school. After high school, too, for that matter. "Back then, I had everything under control. Or thought I did."

"And now?"

"I am one careless mistake away from fired."

"That can't be true." His gaze scanned her corporate persona, from the tight bun all the way through her gray suit and black pumps. She undoubtedly looked as if she had it all together.

"This is just a mirage," she confessed. "Sure, I'm on the corporate fast track, but the better you perform, the more they expect of you. I'm the go-to girl for problems. I'm the go-to girl for—" she almost said layoffs, but stopped herself in time "—for restructuring. I'm the go-to girl for reports that make everything clear."

He blinked. "Wow. You're the go-to schlub. Never expected that."

"What?"

"You know, *that* person. That smart, overachieving schlub that everyone dumps whatever they can on. And the schlub gets it done. Which is why the schlub gets promoted, but also gets—"

"The early heart attack—"

"Or panic attacks."

"Touché. But not everyone can have a brilliant engineering idea, then sell it for zillions." She leaned forward. "I looked you up. You made a fortune in just a few years." He'd figured out some circuit board something that she didn't even understand, but it was revolutionary. He'd built a company, then sold it eight months ago for an incredible amount of money. Now he did some consulting work and played amateur hypnotist on Thursday nights at his brother's bar. "I always knew you were smart, but damn, Jimmy, you've done awesome."

"I'm no stranger to pressure, Nicky," he said softly. "One year ago, I was on the verge of meltdown myself. It's why I sold my company. I couldn't hack it alone and was spending all my time on management—which I hated—rather than R & D."

She sighed, fighting envy. "I was a star in high school 'cause it was easy and I was pretty. In the real world, I have to work hard. And no, I'm not likely to be fired anytime soon, despite my fears. Plus I have enough in the bank to cover a year's mortgage. But that could all change in a minute, and you know it."

He shook his head. "I think you undervalue yourself."

She started to laugh, but it came out more as a choked sob. "You don't know anything about me."

He was silent a long time. Long enough that she brought her eyes back to his, then flickered away only to hop back again. Away and back, a couple times. But he never wavered. He was perfect in his silence and his steady regard, and in the end, she settled enough to hold his gaze.

Finally, he spoke, his voice low and mesmerizing. "Let's change that," he said. "Let's find out more about Nicky."

"You said you were going to hypnotize me."

"I said I'd help you figure out what happened and why."

She swallowed. "We already know—"

"Hush," he said with a tinge of impatience. "I'm the hypnotist. You're the subject. Do you trust me? Can you relax your guard enough to answer my questions? Do as I ask?"

She swallowed, anxiety making her hands clench. "I think so."

"Good. Now we're going to pick a word. You can use that word whenever you want to end things. Just thinking that word will be enough to pull you out, but it's better if you say it aloud."

"A safety word."

"Exactly. You'll always be able to say it. You can stop things whenever you want. Just—"

"Think the word. I mean, say it aloud."

He nodded. "So, any ideas what you want that word to be?"

"Pistachio."

He tilted his head in surprise. "The nut?"

"The ice cream." Then she shrugged. "It's the ice cream I had—"

"Prom night. We went to the café and you ordered pistachio ice cream. I remember."

She smiled. "It…tastes like safety to me. I know that's stupid, but that taste…it's safe."

His expression softened. "That's not stupid at all. In fact, I'm glad I made you feel safe that night."

She flushed and looked away. This was already uncomfortably intimate, and now she'd just confessed something she'd never told anyone before. But then, she'd told Jimmy a ton of things that night that she'd never told anyone before. And the memory made her squirm with nostalgic longing. Everything was so much clearer back in high school.

"Um, can we get on with this?" she asked.

"Sure. But you have to look at me."

She'd been gazing at the subtle texture in his gray carpet, but now her eyes pulled up to his chin. He had a firm chin with a shadow of a beard. It was kinda… rakish. Really sexy.

He touched her cheek. She hadn't even seen his hand move, but she felt the caress all the way to her toes. And just like that, her gaze was locked with his.

"Just remember pistachio. Say it, and you'll feel completely safe. You'll *be* completely safe."

"Pistachio," she whispered, and damn if it didn't work. Just saying the word brought back the warmth of the café, the vinyl seats of the booth, the smell of coffee and burgers in the air. Jimmy sat across from her, the world was on the outside and everything was perfect in that one moment of perfection. And if that weren't weird enough already, her perfect café was sitting right smack-dab in the middle of her island of lusty delight. She knew she was a split second away from sand, sun and hot oil abandon.

"Good," he said, clearly oblivious to how totally turned on she'd suddenly gotten. "Let's begin." He reached behind her and clicked on a light. It was a lamp that he adjusted to form a spotlight onto his left arm. Then, before she could ask what he was doing, he sat back down and lifted a pocket watch. How totally traditional. She would have said the thought, but with a flick of his wrist, he set it spinning, reflecting the light like a strobe.

She wanted to say something, was mentally reaching for some sort of joke or quip that would dismiss the tension she felt coiling in her belly, but she couldn't form the words. Her mind was already embracing the strobing light, emptying of everything but the steady flash.

Click. There it was, her mental off switch. As soon as the power was cut to her brain, everything slipped away—her fears, her tensions, her constant *thinking*. And just like before, her island paradise surrounded her and she felt free, free, free!

"You're smiling," he observed. "Why?"

"No more thinking. Just being. It's wonderful." Was that her voice? Deep. Slow. Sultry, even, in a not-quite-awake way.

"Hmmm. Okay, let's start with the basics. Say your safety word just to make sure it works."

"No."

He frowned. "Why not?"

"I like this. I don't need the word."

"Because it will break you out of the hypnosis?"

"Yes. Mmmmm…" Nicky felt her head tilt back. It was weird the way this worked. She didn't *think* about tilting her head back, then actually do it. She just experienced the sensation of her head dropping back against his lush couch. Then she felt her legs stretch out before her as her chest expanded in a full breath. "Ahhhh," she said as she exhaled. "I can breathe again."

"Good. Now tell me why you followed me home last night."

She rolled her head on the couch to look directly at him. "Because you said to."

He frowned. "So it was the hypnosis."

She laughed, and the sound was throaty and dark. "No. It was because I liked it."

"You liked what we did?"

"Of course."

"But there's something else?"

She stretched her hands high above her head. "Of course."

"What did you like, Nicky? What specifically did you like?"

"I liked being told what to do." Then she peered around her elbow. "I didn't like that you failed to make me come."

He stiffened. "Um, not true. I made you come—"

"From just nipple play alone."

"Ah." He dropped his chin on his hand. "You're right that I failed there. Did you want to try again?"

She took another deep breath and let her arms flop open with a sigh of disgust. "You're not as good at this as you were last night."

"Why?"

She looked at him, and she felt her eyebrows arch in disdain. "Is that a command?"

"Uh...yeah." Then he straightened, lifted his pocket watch again and spun it. What little remained of her mind burned away beneath the strobe. All that was left was this moment, this exact second and his voice as it filled her thoughts. "Nicky," he said sternly, "I command you to tell me why I was better last night than I am now."

"Because last night you told me exactly what to say and do."

"I told you to tell me your fantasy."

"Yes."

"And I told you where to put your hands on the railing."

She smiled. "And to not let go."

"And you like being commanded?"

"Oh, yes."

"Why?" And when she didn't answer at first, he strengthened his tone. "Nicky! Tell me why!"

"All day long, I order people around. Hundreds of employees jump when I say boo, ten thousand reports that tell my bosses what to do. I even order myself around. Sit up straight! Work late! Get it done!"

"And now?"

She grinned and felt her head fall backward again. "Now I don't make any orders. I don't think them up. I just do them."

"And you like that? Being ordered around?" He paused a moment. "Being dominated?"

"Oh, yes." She purred the words.

"And what if I ordered you to do something immoral? Something bad."

She lifted her head, her bottom lip thrust forward into a pout. "You won't, will you?"

"You have your safety word, remember? Will it work?"

She thought about that for a moment. She almost thought the word, but she didn't. It was right there at the edge of her mind, ready and waiting for her to use. But she didn't. She liked where she was.

"Nicky? Would you say the word if you didn't like what I said?"

"Yes."

"Excellent." Then he abruptly narrowed his eyes and spoke in a commanding tone. "Nicky! Tell me the truth now. Is being dominated one of your fantasies?"

She felt her lips curve in a slow smile. She meant to ask for more details. But in this state, she didn't have the ability to question. She simply answered. "Yes."

"How?" he asked.

She simply opened her eyes and looked at him.

"Ah," he said, and she could tell he understood. "That's for me to decide, isn't it?"

"Yes."

"Tell me what you want, Nicky. Tell me exactly what you want me to do."

She arched a brow. "Make me come. Make me orgasm over and over and over. Make me scream your name while you are thick and hard, ramming inside me." She shivered at the delight of it all. "Oh, I want that so very much."

"Oh," he said, and his voice came out as a kind of squeak. Then he cleared his throat. "But I don't think that's what the normal Nicky wants."

She looked back at him, and she saw the torchlight reflected in his eyes. It had the same effect as his watch strobing in front of her. Her mind bled away and she said exactly what she was thinking. "Of course it's what normal Nicky wants. I am Normal Nicky. And Responsible Nicky, too." She grimaced as she referred to her boring persona. "Why do you think I called you? I'm not dumb, you know. I wanted to feel this free again. I want you to try again."

She abruptly leaned forward, dashing close enough to his face to quickly lick his lips. He wasn't expecting it and he drew back with a gasp. But she knew she had affected him. There was a distinct bulge beneath his jeans.

"Uh…" He blinked at her, obviously at war within himself. So she decided to help him out.

"I want to tell you a fantasy, Jimmy."

"Uh…okay."

"I want a master. A sex master. I want him to tell me exactly what to do when and where and how. I want him to decide everything. And I want him to make me come over and over and over again."

He arched a brow at her, but there was hunger in his gaze. "You want me to do all the work, don't you? And take all the responsibility."

She grinned. He understood. "You're an inventor, Jimmy. Invent for me the perfect orgasm."

He stared at her, still undecided. "Is this what you want, Nicky? Is this what you want deep down inside in your most honest self?"

"Oh, yes!" There was no doubt in her mind because there was no need to hide her desires in this island paradise. That's what she most loved about it. No thoughts. No responsibility. Just pleasure.

"But why me, Nicky? Why out of all the men in the world did you come to me?"

She grinned. He was so silly. "Because you make this place, this moment, this feeling. You make it perfect and safe and free." She spread her legs in an obvious invitation. "So will you do it? Will you give me the perfect orgasm?"

8

JIM TRIED TO FORCE his brain to work, but the moment Nicky dared him to give her the most perfect orgasm, his thoughts fuzzed straight out. He tried to keep things sane. He'd tried to explore why she wanted him to do this to her, why she needed to be hypnotized to touch this sexual side of her, why...a thousand whys. But whenever he tried to force himself to think, he came back to: why not?

She was aware. She was articulate. And she'd told him exactly what she wanted. Why not give it to her? Why not show the Nicky of his dreams that he could be more than just the safe loser from down the street. He was strong, he could dominate and he could, by God, be her sexual master. Why not?

"Are you going to regret this in the morning, Nicky? 'Cause you're damn well going to remember it."

She grinned and stretched her arms high above her head, thrusting her breasts toward him in open invitation. "I won't regret a thing," she said, a challenge in every line of her body. "Not if you do it right."

He arched a brow at her. "I think you meant to say, do it right...*master*."

She echoed his pose, arching her own brow back at him. "Do it right, master, *please*."

What more could he say to that? He'd tried to be honorable, he'd tried to keep his mind on task. But this was what she wanted, and he wanted to be the man to give it to her. So he leaned back, thinking about what exactly he should order her to do.

"Take off your thong, Nicky, then go to the back of the couch and bend over."

She straightened, but he held up a hand to stop her. She froze immediately.

"Whenever you hear my command, I want you to say, 'Yes, master.' That way, I'll know this is exactly what you want. You have your other word if you want to stop. Do you understand?"

She grinned, but let her chin dip in a nod. "Yes, master." Then while he sat there and watched, she peeled off her thong right there in front of him. The fabric was wet, the sight going straight to his groin. She wanted this. She wanted it all as she calmly stepped behind the couch. There was plenty of room there so she had space to settle her forearms on the back of the couch, then lift her pert bottom up high.

He straightened off the ottoman, moving slowly to relish this moment. All he had to do was...was... Hell. He had to get some condoms. Did he have any?

"Don't move. I'll be right back."

"Yes, master."

He paused, liking the sound of that. "While I'm gone, strip off your top. I want you naked from the waist up. And...um...start playing with your nipples."

"Yes, master."

He waited long enough to see her pull off her suit jacket. She tossed it aside without a second thought and then went straight to her blouse buttons. He almost groaned at the thought of her doing a strip tease before him, but he had to get condoms. Right now. So he spun on his heel and dashed up the stairs. He had to have some in his bathroom drawer. He had to!

Jackpot! Four left in the box. He grabbed them all and dashed back downstairs. When he rounded the corner, he stopped to appreciate the sight. There was Nicky standing in her heels and skirt, a power executive from the waist down. And from the waist up, her hands were on her breasts, her head was thrown back in abandon and her mouth was open on a gasp of sheer delight. She was playing with her nipples just as he'd instructed.

The sight was beyond incredible. Sure, she was a beautiful woman. What man wouldn't go nuts to see a woman doing that to herself? But what made him stop dead in his tracks was her enjoyment. Even from across the room, he could see that Nicky wasn't thinking about anything else. She wasn't planning her next move, wondering what he would like or even thinking about what he might do to her next. She was simply absorbed in the exquisite sensations of her fingers pulling at her nipples, of thumbing and twisting them. Her breath came in short pants, her skin was flushed a rosy pink, and he could see her shudder with the early signs of orgasm. Good God, she was going to make herself come! And he was going to follow just by watching her!

"Stop!" he ordered.

Her hands froze.

"Lean over the couch and lift your bottom as high into the air as you can."

"Yes, master." She did as he ordered.

He walked slowly around her, seeing the way her breasts were smashed by the back of the couch. Leaning around, he adjusted the cushions so that her hands were planted higher and her breasts dangled. He reached out and tweaked a pointed nipple and was pleased when she gasped in reaction.

"Does this make you wet?" He could smell the answer in the air, but he wanted to hear her say it.

"Yes, master."

"Let's see." He stepped behind her, stroking his hands up the outside of both her legs. Her skirt crumpled as he moved, and in the end, he flipped it up over her butt to reveal her perfect ass right there before him.

Each globe was white and firm and gorgeous. He smoothed his hand over her slowly, feeling the softness of her skin, knowing that her legs trembled.

"Widen your legs."

"Yes, master."

"Just like that. Don't let your knees go out."

"Yes, master."

He stroked his knuckle over her from the back to the front, taking his time in her wet center, then pushing forward to press rhythmically against her clit. She moaned, but didn't move.

He did it again and again to her, but by the third time, his restraint was at an end. He had to be in her. He'd been thinking about how he could do her since he was a teenager, but it had been a nonstop fantasy since last night. In fact, he'd spent the day imagining just this moment.

So without further subtlety, he stripped off his pants and rolled on the condom. And he as worked, he wondered exactly how far his control of her went. How far could he push her until she cried, "pistachio"? At the moment, he didn't care. The condom was on. Her body was right there before him. He stepped up behind her, taking one moment to stroke her with his dick, in part for pleasure and in part to know exactly where everything was.

She moaned again, and the sound sent him over the cliff. He slammed into her. God, she was so wet and so tight, and nothing had ever felt more perfect than this.

"Don't come," he ordered. His words were for himself. He was deep inside her, and he wanted to preserve the moment, but she answered as if it were an order.

"Yes, master."

He leaned over her, far enough to stroke her from shoulder to hip. Then he pushed upward to fondle her breasts. He lifted them, squeezed them, even rolled her nipples between his fingers. She shuddered beneath him. Her internal muscles gripped him tight. She was on the verge.

"Don't come," he ordered. "Not until I tell you to."

"Yes, master."

She was so close. He wondered if she would hold out. He wondered if *he* could hold out. Not long, he realized. For both of them. So he slid his hands down to her hips and gripped her there. Then he slid slowly out, almost all the way, before slamming back in.

Oh God, she felt great. He did it again. Out slowly, then in as hard and fast as he could thrust.

"Tell me how it feels to you. How do I feel?"

"You're thick. Huge," she breathed.

He slammed in again.

"I feel you. So deep."

"Do you want more?"

"Oh yes, master."

That was it. Her voice so breathy ended any semblance of control. "Now! Come now!"

She did. She convulsed with a gasped cry, and he lost all consciousness beyond the final slam into her. He was coming, pushing every piece of himself into her. Pleasure exploded across his senses, like a wave of ecstasy, and it rolled through him to crash into her. She was still convulsing. Her back was arched, her mouth open.

Then her upper body fell forward. She lay there across his couch, her entire body limp. He was sprawled across her back, his heartbeat thundering in his ears.

"That was good," he said as much to himself as to her. But she answered, her words flowing through her body into his.

"Yes, master," she murmured.

He smiled, unable to stop himself from pressing long tender kisses into her back. He stayed like that for long minutes. The orgasm had been more intense than he'd ever experienced.

"It was perfect," he said as he marveled at the smooth expanse of her skin.

"No, master."

He froze. "What? What did you say?"

She lifted her head, lengthening her back. Despite his intentions, he slid out of her. "No, master."

"No, it wasn't a perfect orgasm?"

She twisted to look at him, and her expression was both honest and a challenge. "No, master, that was *not* a perfect orgasm."

Huh, he thought as he rocked back on his heels. Then he thought over what they had done. Okay, so he'd been dreaming of taking Nicky over the back of a couch since he was old enough to think about using a couch that way.

But that was *his* fantasy, not hers. Ergo, what they'd just done was for him, not her.

"But you enjoyed it, right?"

She dimpled prettily. "Yes, master."

"But it wasn't perfect."

"No, master."

"Well," he said slowly, his mind spinning furiously. "I guess I'll just have to try harder." After all, he still had three more condoms in the box, and it was still early on a Friday night.

Her mouth tilted up in a soft smile. "Yes, master."

9

NICKY SAT RIGIDLY UPRIGHT on James's couch. He hadn't said much before he disappeared. She was to wait for his return. She was to wait naked until he returned. He hadn't said anything beyond that. She probably could stretch out on the couch and watch headline news if she wanted.

She didn't.

It was very odd, she realized, this arousal that simmered through her blood and liquified her belly. In her normal life, the last thing she would ever do is sit still without her cell phone, without access to e-mail, without thinking or planning or managing. This whole situation was very bizarre, said the tiny, thinking portion of her brain.

So she turned it off. She consciously closed her eyes, put herself firmly in the middle of her hot tropical beach, and let everything else just disappear. There wasn't a conscious *click* in her head, but the effect was the same. She was a woman stripped of all ability to function on her own. Her naked body was a reflection of that internal state. Her doll-like position on the couch was also a manifestation of the blank state of her mind. Her only thought was anticipation.

That, and that she was probably making a wet spot on his couch.

He returned while her eyes were still closed. She heard him enter the room, but she didn't want to look and disturb the near silence of the moment.

"Don't move," he ordered.

"Yes, master," she whispered.

"I like seeing you like that. Except for the shoes. Put your shoes back on."

"Yes, master." He clearly had a thing for black pumps. She leaned down and slipped them on. They were rounded-toe pumps with a flirty bow. Cute, but serviceable, and not so high she feared she'd break an ankle on a factory floor.

She frowned at the thought. Her mind was trying to gain a foothold again, and she had no desire to go there. So she settled back on the couch, her eyes closed once again, and she pulled up the island heat. Between one breath and the next, her mind blanked to nothing.

"Just to be clear again, Nicky, you're enjoying being forced, right?"

"Yes, master."

"But forced how? Do you like it rough? Cold, even?"

She tilted her head, wondering. She didn't know, and frankly, she didn't like thinking about it. This was something for him to decide. Then she would decide afterward what she thought.

"Keep your eyes closed," he said, his voice growing louder as he moved closer. "And answer without thinking. Have you ever done anything like this with another man?"

"No, master."

"Have you ever explored any of your fantasies before?"

"No, master."

"None of them? Why not?"

Questions, questions. She didn't like that his questions made her think. That defeated the whole purpose of being here in her island pleasure place. But he'd told her to answer quickly without considering, so she let her mind blank as the words flowed. "Bad girl, bad Nicky. Have you done your homework? Have you finished the report? Have you paid off your debts?"

"Hmmm," he said. He was standing in front of her now. She could feel his island god heat. "That's the truth, but that's not the whole truth, is it?"

"No, master."

"So what is the truth?"

"Nicky has bad taste in men." She was beginning to squirm in her seat. All these questions were cutting too close to thought, forcing her to a place that wasn't her island paradise. And yet, in a bizarre way, it felt right that he ask. Jimmy always asked questions, he always cut to the heart of things. That was one of the reasons she liked him so.

"Stop moving," he said firmly from right in front of her.

She stilled. Then she felt his hand on her face, his fingers gentle as he stroked her cheek, her jaw, her mouth. His thumb lingered on her lower lip, brushing back and forth, back and forth in a mesmerizing motion. "You're safe here, Nicky," he said, his voice low and deep. "You're also smart, capable and beautiful. You deserve a man who knows that and reveres you for it."

His words settled into her bones, strong and powerful

because on this island he was god. And because he was god, her confidence strengthened, her core grew stronger, and—oddly enough—she settled deeper under his spell. She liked it here. She liked what he said. And most of all, she liked how she felt when he touched her.

"So you want to explore, Nicky?"

"Yes, master." Inside she was smiling. Enough thinking, enough talking. She wanted to know what he would do to her next.

He slipped a blindfold over her eyes. It was satin, she realized, and cool. It caught on one of the pins of her updo and she felt him push her bun left and right as he began delving into her hair.

"How many pins are in here?" he groused.

Then it was down and the satin blindfold tightened against her eyes. Her hair was flattened against her scalp, clearly knotted in places, probably an unholy mess, but it didn't matter. She was what he commanded, and she smiled at the thought.

Her right nipple exploded with sensation. He had flicked it with his thumb, and she gasped in reaction. But she didn't move. She wasn't allowed to move.

"Your nipples are tight. Are you cold?" he asked.

Her legs were abruptly shoved apart and she was pushed back against the cushions of the couch.

"It's hot here," he said.

Good god, that felt amazing. She was spread open. Would he—

He shoved his fingers inside her.

Yes!

"It's hot here, too." He spoke casually, almost as if he were indifferent. Except she knew he wasn't. She knew it!

He moved his fingers around, and her bottom tightened in reaction. She was lifting up to him, begging for more. Then he withdrew, and she mourned the loss. But she didn't say anything. She'd been commanded to be silent, and that completed the fantasy. If she couldn't speak, then there was no need to think of something to say.

"Stand up."

She did. He didn't help her. It was a little awkward given that she couldn't see, but she managed it. Then he took her arm and tugged her forward. He wasn't forceful, neither was he tender. He simply led and she followed. Her heels sunk into the carpet, then they clicked on tile, but not the hallway kind. This sounded more like…kitchen. She was in the kitchen.

She heard a door open. It was a heavy one. She knew because she could hear the suction as he pulled it open, and there was a brush of cold air as if he were taking her outside.

Outside? Naked? She tensed, pulling back when he wanted her to go forward.

"Nicky? I want you to move forward."

There was a question underneath his order. He was really asking if she trusted him to keep her safe, no matter what game awaited her on the other side of the door. And below that question was the deeper one. Did she want to stay in this blissful, thought-free state?

Yes to both. She trusted him and she didn't want to think right now. Perhaps never again. So she took a step forward, but he stopped her by tightening his grip on her arm.

"Say it. Say yes, master, or the other word."

"Yes, master."

"All right, then. This way."

He pulled her forward. She stepped as he directed, but

her heel caught on something at the threshold and she stumbled. Her body lurched forward, and she squeaked in alarm. She reached out with her hands, but already knew she wouldn't be fast enough. And she couldn't see!

He caught her around the waist. She'd thought of him as just a disembodied voice, as a hand on her arm dragging her forward. But now he was a man, his body strong and hard as one arm wrapped around her waist and the other supported her front just beneath her breasts. She could feel the muscles of his forearms, the hard press of his fingers on her ribs, and then the solid bulk of his whole body as he braced her against him so that she could find her footing.

It took a long time. She was surprised at how disorienting losing her sight was, and so she fumbled at getting her feet under her. The edge of her heel slid on the flooring, and she realized it was concrete. Like in a garage. But that was a distant impression that did little to penetrate the feel of his body supporting hers.

He wore his same clothing, an old tee and soft jeans. He liked comfort, she could tell, because the fabric was gentle on her naked body. Her head had banged against his shoulder, but as she stood, she was able to lift herself higher until her forehead brushed his chin. Or perhaps he leaned into her, tilting his head so that he prolonged their contact?

She didn't know, and she found she didn't care. He was holding her, touching her, and each sensation built one on top of the other until he was the wall against everything else. He was her world, and he made her safe. That's what she remembered even as he pulled away from her until she was standing alone again.

"Are you all right?" he asked.

"Yes, master," she returned.

"Then come forward and climb onto this table."

He touched her lower back with a light brush of her fingers. It was enough to give her direction, but not tell her where he was. It didn't matter. She now knew he would be there if she needed him. Right now, she didn't, and so she stepped forward to touch a cold Formica table.

"Up on your knees."

"Yes, master."

She fumbled her way up onto all fours. The toes of her shoes had little traction on this table, and the Formica was hard on her knees. Her fingers found the edges—just a little wider than shoulder width—and she wrapped her fingers around the lip and gripped tight. She couldn't keep her knees together, but she wasn't spread completely wide. She settled into a stable pose, feeling her breasts sway beneath her.

She'd barely gotten settled when he pushed a finger deep inside her. She arched and gasped in reaction, but it didn't dislodge him. She didn't want to, especially as he wiggled a bit, pulled out, then pushed two fingers back in.

"God, you are so ready, Nicky, I could do you again, just like this."

"Yes, master," she gasped, hoping he would do just that. He was still plunging into her, moving his fingers as he wanted while she arched her back more, hoping he would find something to do with her clit.

"I could, but I don't think that would be the perfect orgasm. At least not for you, would it?"

"No, master."

"Very well, then. Let's keep exploring." He withdrew from inside her, though he stroked his wet fingers around her bottom, and up along her spine. She felt his other hand on her right breast, idly toying with her.

She waited, her body tight with anticipation and wet with desire. But she didn't think. In fact, she was beginning to believe she would never think again. Her only task was to wait and experience.

Though she still managed a mew of distress when he lifted his hands away from her completely.

"Turn over. I want you to lie down on your back."

"Yes, master." The awkward flip over on this narrow table made her heart beat faster and her breath catch. But she accomplished the task without help. She now lay on her back on the hard table.

"Lift your head."

She did as she was bid.

"Now lie down."

He'd placed a thick, rolled towel under her neck. It didn't provide much cushion, but it did make the situation less uncomfortable. And while she was relaxing into the towel, she felt something cold click around her left wrist. Her hand was down by her hip, and he jerked it abruptly upright so she could feel the cold bite of a handcuff on her wrist. Then he let it drop to land on the table. A moment later, she felt another cuff slap around her other wrist. She was now bound to the table.

"Widen your knees," he ordered.

Her legs had been pushed demurely together, but now she rolled her knees outward.

"Wide," he said. "As wide as you can."

"Yes, master," she murmured, then tried to push her heel into the table for leverage. It slid uselessly away. She had no traction at all. So she simply tightened her outer thighs, shivering slightly as the cold air hit every part of her groin. Her legs were spread wide, but it required her lower stomach muscles to keep them up in the air.

"Nice flexibility," he commented, and she felt warmed by the compliment. Then she heard some strange noises. He was doing something to the table, but she couldn't tell what. And her abdominals were starting to tremble. She might be flexible, but it had been a long while since she'd taken the time to do stomach crunches.

She felt his hands, large and warm on her right leg. Then something thick and hard like leather wrapped around her thigh, just above her knee. He shifted, bracing her knee against his stomach. She could tell by the way his jeans provided a lip to rest her weight on. She felt the strap tighten and buckle. Then he released her leg so that it dangled off the side of the table.

He moved away, not touching her anymore. Her lower back arched slightly with her leg hanging off the side. And when he repeated the process on her other side, she ended up fully stretched, her breasts pushed to the sky with her groin open and her legs dangling uselessly over the edge.

"Try to move off the table," he ordered.

"Yes, master." She did, and it was impossible. Her hands were shackled, her legs spread open. She couldn't get any leverage anywhere. The most she could do was grip the table tight enough that her thighs hurt where the edge cut in against her flesh.

"You may stop now. You are cuffed and bound to this table, Nicky. I can do anything I want to you, and you can't stop me."

She could, though. She knew she could with her one word, but she didn't say it. She didn't even think it.

"You are completely and wholly at my mercy," he continued. "This is what you wanted, isn't it?"

"Yes, master."

"Perfect." There was the rustle of fabric and then the creak. Was he getting on the table? Yes, she definitely thought so.

She felt heat and movement. His forearms braced on either side of her head, pulling a bit at her hair. She felt his groin settle on her mons, the wet feel of latex a bizarre contrast to the heat of his body. He was naked and lying on top of her, and the skin-to-skin heat was wonderful.

"Wrap your legs around me," he said.

"Yes, master." Her voice was breathy, her blood pounding through her body. She strained her legs, but it was hard to move with the restraints above her knees. He had to help her until she settled her calves on the back of his.

But then he didn't do anything. Absolutely nothing at all.

"Nicky," he said softly, his voice so close that she could feel the heat of his breath on her ear. "Do you trust me?"

"Absolutely."

"Then I think you have excellent taste in men."

She smiled, her lips curving as she reflected on his words. Was he right? Was she as smart as she pretended? In this place the answer was a definite yes.

And then she felt him shift. Between one breath and the next he pushed himself inside her. She arched in reaction, but she couldn't move far. She was so wet, he went in easily, but god he filled her. She was stretched from inside and weighted down from above. He completely surrounded her, and it was wonderful.

Then he withdrew in a long pull before slamming back into her. She felt the impact like a body blow, hard and full and perfect. The impact filled her mind and body, ratcheting everything tighter.

He did it again. Oh yes, again! Her breath shuddered, her body tightened. Once more and then...

He didn't slam in again. He withdrew abruptly and stayed away. The emptiness was a huge loss, but she still felt his weight pressing her hips down. "Lick me!" he ordered. "And suck. Lightly."

She extended her tongue, startled to find his chest right above her mouth. He stretched and moved, but apparently not where he wanted. He moved again. Her tongue rolled over muscle and flesh and through chest hair. Then she felt it: the hard nub of his nipple. She concentrated there, flicking her tongue over it, even sucking it as best as she could. When he groaned above her, she knew she had done well.

Then he was gone, his chest pulled away. She barely had time to process that he was gone when she felt his penis thrust hard into her again. Big. Thick. Abrupt. She cried out at the impact.

He was grinding into her with every thrust. His motions were hard, his every gasp seemingly wrenched from him.

She had done this to him. She had brought him to this mindless place of rutting, and she loved it. The slam into her felt so right. She tightened her legs but she couldn't get a grip. She wanted to come. She needed to...

Her belly tightened, but it was too late.

"Agh!" he roared as he released into her. She felt his contractions, knew each individual pulse of his organ as she tightened around him. She so wanted to follow him, but she couldn't. She didn't. And so she whimpered, even as she gloried in his steady pulse inside her.

He collapsed on top of her, his groan trembling from

him into her. It was hard to breathe, and the table was going to cut off her circulation soon. She hoped he didn't fall asleep there on top of her, but how wonderful if she had just brought him to exhaustion. The accomplishment warmed her, even as worries began to lap at the edges of her mind. Should she say something? Should she wake him?

She needn't have wondered. Within moments, he took a deep shuddering breath and stirred. "You're going to kill me," he whispered into her ear. "But I'm going to die happy."

Then with a heave, he pushed himself up and off of her. The move was abrupt and devastating. She could finally breathe, but the loss of his heat and his presence created an ache of loneliness.

"I didn't mean to do that," he said, his tone regretful. "I just meant to tease you, but you're so damn beautiful, I got carried away."

She didn't speak. She didn't know what to say except that she liked that she could distract him, that she could bring him to that place of mindlessness just like her own.

"Was that a perfect orgasm?" he asked.

"No, master."

"Of course not. Because you didn't even orgasm, did you?"

"No, master."

"So let's fix that. But first I'll have to wash you off."

She exhaled slowly, waiting for the brush of cloth. Her legs had flopped off the edge again, so she was wide open for his ministrations. Maybe the cloth would do what he hadn't—

Water dripped on her groin, and she cried out in

surprise, arching away though she couldn't go far. Instead, she felt the steady stream flow on her inside thigh. Cold. Shocking. But before she could register more than that, he pressed his forearm on her belly, pinning her down.

"Don't move, Nicky. Stay right there."

"Yes, master," she said. She relaxed her thighs and her back. The tension was beginning to hurt anyway. Then she heard noises that she didn't understand. He was close, but not touching her.

And the stream of water moved. Up her thigh, into her mons, and then…right onto her. And if she had any doubt as to his intention, his fingers touched her, lifting her flesh away such that the stream slid right over her clit.

She gasped, feeling overwhelmed by the sensations. Cold water flowing over her. Her nipples tightened in reaction. In fact, her entire body clenched at the icy feel.

Then it was abruptly gone to be replaced by a curling heat through her groin. His tongue, she realized, stroking. Warming. Thick and long as he tongued her flesh to life again. Then harder and pointy as he swirled around her clit.

After the frigid cold, this was incredible. Her body tensed, her belly tightened. She was building fast to orgasm. Just one more…

Ice hit her clit. Not the steady stream of water, but a square-shaped ice cube, pressed right against her flesh. She yelped and recoiled, but it didn't help. He followed her, neither moving the hard form against her to push her over the orgasmic edge nor easing it away to keep the cold from numbing everything. At least it was melting.

And while her thoughts were still on the slowly shrinking cube of ice, she felt his mouth on her nipple. She hadn't even realized he'd moved until the suction began on her breast. He was tonguing her, warming her torso while part of her remained ice-cold. The dichotomy was surprisingly exciting. Hot and cold. Bound and free. And alive. So very alive. As if every nerve in her body was hyperalert, ready for any sensation—every sensation!—to explode across her mind.

He stopped with her right breast, leaving it puckered and wet. The cold on her nipple was a dim echo of the cold below. The ice had fallen away or melted completely—she didn't know. She didn't really care. It was all glorious sensation.

And then there was more.

10

"NICKY," HE WHISPERED. His lips were right by her ear, and his heated breath fluttered her hair deep enough to warm her scalp.

"Yes, master?"

"Nicky, I'm going to ask you some questions now. If you answer honestly, you'll get a reward. Do you understand?"

"Yes, master."

"And even more important, I want you to remember these questions, okay? I'd like to talk to you about them later. After...well, after tonight, if you want."

"Yes, master."

He dropped a quick kiss on her lips. The movement was so abrupt that it was over by the time she thought to respond.

"Okay, Nicky. First question. Does being bound like this excite you sexually?"

"Yes, master."

She felt his hand stroke her cheek, caressing over her jaw and up toward her eye. He had to stop at the edge of the blindfold, but then stroked back down toward her ear.

"Describe the sensations to me, please," he said. "How does this arousal feel?"

She frowned, but strove to answer. In this place of non-thought, she had no inhibition about speaking of these things. She simply began a head-to-toe catalog. "My scalp is tight—it almost tingles. My mouth is dry, my lips feel swollen. And I can breathe. Fully, deeply. But every breath I take makes my breasts bigger, tighter. And my nipples are wet and cold and full and hard and I don't know. They want more."

She felt his hand then, stroking and shaping her left breast. There didn't seem to be any purpose in his touch, just a casual lift and caress, but it was as if he'd stirred the embers of a fire that was only starting to cool. She drew in a breath and arched her back as best as she could. She loved what he did.

"Keep going, Nicky. What else do you feel?"

"Wide open. My legs are spread and there is wetness everywhere."

"Are you cold? Do you need a blanket?"

"No. My belly feels so liquid, as if everything is soft. Like warmed butter. But it's growing hard again."

"Hard is unpleasant?"

"Hard is…cold. Rigid."

He left her breast, and she sighed in dismay. Then she felt his tongue on her groin. His tongue was thick and warm as he lapped a long stroke from her base to her clit. Each stroke had her tightening her butt, pulling open her thighs, lifting as much as possible to his mouth. But he was leisurely. Again, he stirred the fire without seeming to have a destination in mind.

A ripple began from his tongue, a tiny wave that

rolled up her belly but stopped at her diaphragm. It was only a precursor and it was only one.

"More," she murmured. "I want more."

He stopped. "Then you have to keep answering, Nicky. Do you have to be bound on this table to enjoy it?"

"Yes."

"Could I not just do this to you in a bed?"

"No."

"Why?"

"I don't know."

He released his breath in a huff. He'd left her groin, but had one hand high on her left thigh, a single source of heat especially as he began to knead the flesh there. She wasn't used to anyone pushing deeply into the skin there, into the muscles that pulled with the movements of his thumb. But it added to the sensations, and she felt her entire focus center on what he did.

"You are bound and blindfolded, Nicky. I could bring others into this room and you could do nothing about it. Does that excite you?"

"Yes," she whispered.

"So you'd like to have a man on each of your breasts, another holding you open with yet another man pumping into you?"

"Yes." She was panting at the thought.

"What about spanking?"

She blinked and didn't answer.

"Nicky, does that excite you?"

"I don't know." She had never tried pain as a sexual aid. Without this blank state, she would never have allowed herself to think of it before. But now, under his spell, she had the freedom to consider anything, to do anything.

She felt him press a kiss at the very top of her thigh where leg met lower abdominals in a long indent of very sensitive flesh. His lips lingered there, and he even used his teeth to graze the skin. She shivered at the feel, her moan releasing naturally and openly.

"What is sex usually like for you? Without the hypnosis."

"Nonexistent," she answered.

"But it must have happened sometime. You weren't a virgin, were you?"

"No."

"Then what was sex like before?"

"Directed," she said. The answer came out as all her answers did in this place: without prior thought. The first thing that came into her head without censorship or even understanding.

"Directed?" he asked. "How so?"

"I tell him what to do and how. Occasionally I let him pick the position."

"You're in charge, then," he said.

"Yes, master."

"But you're not now."

"No, master."

"And you like it better this way."

She smiled. "Much better."

She flexed toward him, hoping he would reward her now. He did, but only absently. His fingers sunk into her. She had felt this from him before, the thrust of fingers that he wiggled inside her. The roll of his thumb around her clit. But in this place, there was only now, and so this was as exciting as it was before, as powerful a build to orgasm as before. She ached for him to keep doing it.

But again he stopped, and she whimpered as he withdrew from her.

"You have done very well, Nicky, and so now I'm going to give you a gift. I'm going to tell you an image for you to hold in your thoughts. You're going to live it, to experience it just as I direct. Do you understand?"

"Yes, master."

"I want you to pretend that you are a virgin sacrifice in an ancient society. A beautiful young girl with a perfect body. You are being brought naked before the high priest—me."

As he spoke, his words painted a picture for her. She saw herself not as Nicky, but as a young woman, innocent as she never was. But in this moment, in this place, she was sweet. Open. Vulnerable.

"Are we at the volcano?" she asked. "On the island?"

He paused a moment. "The volcano where you threw your cell phone in?"

"Yes."

"Yes, we are. We're right there, beside the volcano, and you're naked. You're naked, but you are not afraid as acolytes tie you to this table and spread you open before me. Is this what you are experiencing, Nicky?"

"Yes, master." Some tiny part of her realized that her voice was higher than before, younger sounding.

"The high priest comes to you, Nicky. He is going to kiss you on the lips, and in that moment, a goddess spirit will enter you. You will be both virginal and pure, but also a goddess, mature and ripe. And as a goddess, your task is simply to be adored. To be touched and worshiped and given pleasure. Do you understand?"

"Yes, master."

And then he did it. He pressed his mouth to hers. He touched his tongue to the seam of her lips, stroking them open slowly, then invading her more fully. And as his tongue thrust into her, she felt something else happen. Expanding in a wave of delight, she became a woman in the body of a young girl. She was powerful, she was eternal, and she was manifested on earth so that the humans could worship her.

He ended the kiss. The transformation was complete. She arched her neck and closed her eyes in total relaxation.

"Adore me," she commanded. Her voice was deep with resonance, and it was all that was needed.

"Two acolytes apply themselves to your breasts."

She felt them, a hand on each breast. One had more skill than the other, but each manipulated and stroked her breasts with adequate attention. Then there was a change: a mouth on one breast, a hand still on the other as it twisted her nipple. The sensations were lovely, and every stroke, every caress was an act of worship which she accepted as her due.

She knew she was still bound, her hands down by her sides. It didn't matter. She had no intention of moving. It was their worship of her and she would put no effort into directing it.

"They continue one at each breast, Nicky. Another strokes your neck and face. Kissing you sometimes. Caressing you at others. Do you feel it all?"

"Yes, high priest," she answered. Her nipples still tingled, her breasts rose and fell with each caress. And now her face and neck felt sensations as well. A silky fabric brushed across her chest. Then fingers and lips. "Your worship is pleasing to me."

"Excellent. But you deserve more."

She did not bother to agree or disagree. He would perform as he willed.

"A line of men waits, praying for their turn to adore

you. They each want to give you pleasure, for that is their greatest joy. But I am the high priest, and only I am allowed to penetrate you."

She didn't answer beyond a flick of a single finger. She would allow his penetration.

"Your orgasms will begin the moment I enter you, but they will not end with me. When I am done, others will step to kiss you, caress you, to bring you to orgasm again and again because that is our greatest joy." Then he paused, and she felt his hand stroke her thighs. "May I begin, goddess?"

"You may."

He filled her. Thick and hot, his member entered her. She gloried in the exquisite hardness of him. She found pleasure in the repeated thrust of his bulk against her. And as he had predicted, the waves of pleasure began with his first stroke.

From her belly outward, the wave began. Pleasure like expanding ripples on a pond. The first was small, but each successive ripple grew in size and intensity. Soon he had built enough momentum for the wave to engulf her. She contracted with him—around him— opening only as he withdrew, tightening again when he thrust deep inside her.

A wave of ecstasy engulfed her, enveloping every part of her in an explosion of joy.

Another wave, another explosion. Someone screamed.

Her priest shuddered and released. She knew it in only a dim part of her awareness.

"Here are the others," he rasped against her belly. "More and more, a line of hundreds of men come to adore you," he said. "The first one is young and blond.

Ripped abs, wide shoulders and he says he has worshiped you all his life."

She felt the boy put his mouth to her clit. She felt him stroke her to climax and she was pleased as the wave roared through her body. She knew she had given the boy such joy.

"The next man is large. A powerful man with a powerful body. He says you have brought his life meaning."

This time the tongue thrusts were harsh against her sensitized clit. But she knew this was what he wanted, and she took his adoration as her due. She crested for him as well.

On and on it went, man after man with the high priest's voice her only framework to wave after wave of worship. She lost all awareness of time. And in the end, her virgin body gave out.

She collapsed into exhaustion and the goddess was forced to depart. Her last words before she slipped away were to the high priest. "Next time," she said, "the girl must be stronger. I would like you to have me twice."

11

JIM JERKED AWAKE. He'd been doing that all night, slamming into alertness, only to realize that it was still the middle of the night, Nicky was still asleep beside him on his bed, and that he really needed to get some rest. Especially since he had no idea how today's "morning after" with Nicky was going to go.

He glanced at the clock—6:42. He looked down at her. Her hair was a bit of a mess, fat curls going every which way, some in clumps, other in wispy strands. Her face was slack in sleep, and he saw bits of something shimmery around her eyes. The remains of yesterday's makeup, he realized. Her lips were open, her breathing deep, but no snoring. That was nice. And then there was her naked shoulder, the tops of her naked breasts, and her bare arm curled up beneath her pillow.

All in all, a beautiful sight. He set his head back down on his pillow and wondered at his conclusion. Individually, the details of her appearance were rather unattractive. But put together in the whole package that was Nicky, she was stunningly beautiful to him. Just lying here next to her made him feel special, like a warm thrill trembled somewhere beneath the surface of his skin. Every moment that she lay beside him, something deep in his heart was doing a happy dance.

He sighed. He needed to think, not lay here mooning over her. He'd gotten several clues into Nicky's psyche last night, and he wanted to figure out as much as possible about her before she woke up. He knew that she had two rather distinct personas. The first was Executive Nicky, as he mentally dubbed the gray-suited woman who was permanently attached to her PDA/cell phone. She was the one who orchestrated everything in her life. Even sex, apparently. She ordered everyone around including herself. Executive Nicky seemed to be afraid that if she let up in any way for even a moment, then disaster would strike. She'd lose her job, her home, her everything. He knew for sure that Executive Nicky didn't want to acknowledge that the other Nicky, Sexy Nicky, even existed. Executive Nicky would never even imagine the things that Sexy Nicky did. And if she did, she'd never, ever admit to it.

The question was why? Why was Executive Nicky so strong? Why did it have to take hypnotism for Sexy Nicky to come out? He'd caught another clue when she said she had terrible taste in men. He knew that had been true in high school. He'd been there prom night rescuing her from the drunken captain of the wrestling team. But could one bad choice in high school color the entire rest of her life? Maybe. Executive Nicky didn't tolerate any screwups, her own most especially. But did Nicky not trust herself because of a single bad boyfriend, or was there more to it? How many bad choices had she made?

He wanted to ask her these questions. He wanted to explore them with her and help her get to Sexy Nicky as often as possible. With him, hopefully. But how did he keep Executive Nicky from blowing a gasket while they searched for the answer? Sure, he could keep hypnotizing her, but that really felt like cheating. Sexy Nicky was great for a night. Or a hundred nights. But in the end, he'd like to have a relationship with a whole woman. He was still pondering the problem thirty-seven minutes later when her eyes fluttered open.

She had pretty eyes. Rich brown. Light behind oak— sturdy, beautiful and filled with life. She blinked twice and a dreamy look came into them.

"Good morning," he whispered with his most winning smile. "Can I get you anything? Coffee? Tea?" *Me?* "Or would you prefer to sleep a little longer?"

Her eyes widened farther, and her head rose slightly off the pillow. Her gaze slipped past him to his room. Then she looked back at him and something changed. Her mouth opened slightly and her eyes alternately narrowed and widened. It wasn't hard to guess what was happening. She was struggling to hold on to her dreamy joy, but the pull of reality was too strong. He watched helplessly as panic crept into her expression. One moment she was a sleeping princess. The next, terrified tigress. Crap.

She was going to bolt. He could see it in every line of her body. He had a second, maybe two, before she leaped out of bed and ran out of his life forever.

"Oh, no…" she whispered.

He pounced. It wasn't so much a plan as an event that his body did while his brain scrambled to catch up. But before either of them realized it, he had flattened her on her back, her wrists were pinned by his hands, and her legs were trapped by his own. And that happy dance under his skin relocated to his dick…which was really happy to be pressed hot and hard against her belly.

She gasped, and his mouth scrambled to catch up to the rest of him. "Don't freak, Nicky."

Her mouth was open, but no sound came out. Panic still tightened her features. So he consciously dropped his voice to its most soothing, most mesmerizing.

"Everything's okay, Nicky. You're safe. You're safe with me."

She swallowed and some of the horror receded from her eyes. "Are you trying to hypnotize me again?" she asked. Her voice came out weak, but it sounded like an attempt at a joke. That was progress.

He matched it with his own weak attempt at a smile. "I just didn't want you screaming."

She swallowed. "Not screaming here."

No, she wasn't. But she also wasn't looking calm or relaxed. In fact, if he had to bet, she was already planning her escape route. "Please don't run, Nicky. I'd like to talk."

"No promises. I'm feeling pretty freaked right now," she said with a shrug. But that brought his groin in intimate contact with hers. And given that they were both naked, she abruptly froze. Unfortunately, he wasn't so controlled. He pushed harder against her without intending to while pleasure temporarily overrode his brain.

"Jimmy…" she breathed.

Swear to god, he couldn't tell if that was hunger or a warning. His brain just wasn't working.

"Jimmy," she repeated. "You don't have a condom on. I'm not on the pill. I could get pregnant."

It was a measure of how far gone he was that the idea of her carrying his child wasn't the least bit of a deterrent.

"You said I was safe with you, Jimmy. I don't want to get pregnant right now. Jimmy—"

"I know! I know! I'm getting off."

Her eyes widened, and he almost laughed despite the situation.

"Not getting off that way. I'm going to get off you. Just don't run, okay? I know you're mentally halfway down the block…" He glanced at her guarded expression. "Or across the world from me, but I'd really just like to talk to you. Please don't run."

"I won't," she said, but they both knew it was a lie, because she flushed. "At least not right away." She gave him a rueful look. "I'm trying to be honest here. I'm… uh…really freaked right now."

"I understand." And he did. He just hoped they could get past the panic. "I'm getting off now."

He waited a moment, mostly to get his rampaging testosterone under control. He really, really wanted her. And she was right there. But he managed to hog-tie his inner Neanderthal, and rolled off of her. He landed on his back with a groan. Lord, he did *not* like being chivalrous in the morning. But Nicky was too important for him to give in to his baser instincts. And as he lay there, he heard her climb out of bed.

"Nicky—"

"I'm just going to the bathroom. I'm not running. I'm just…the bathroom." He heard her go in there and quietly shut the door.

She took a long time in there. Plenty of time for him to figure out what to say to her. But he still hadn't a clue by the time she finally emerged, her face pale and freshly scrubbed, so his only thought was to go for honesty.

"We had fun last night, Nicky. You had fun! Forget

how you think you *ought* to feel. Forget Ms. Uptight Executive Nicky. Just be yourself for a moment, without the burden of what you ought to think and ought to do. We're two consenting adults and there's no reason to bolt."

He saw her struggle with her answer. She had wrapped herself in his bathrobe, which was two sizes too large for her, but it still didn't hide the clench in her muscles. He'd managed to pull on his sweatpants, and sat on the bed staring at her in a weird echo of yesterday morning.

"Why?" She said the word so softly that he almost didn't hear it. But he did, and moreover, he knew what she was asking. Why did she enjoy something she clearly thought was one step away from depraved?

"That's what I wanted to ask you. You liked being tied up, didn't you?"

She swallowed, then she dipped her chin. Again, the motion was so tiny, he might have missed it, but he was watching very closely.

"You liked being dominated. You liked calling me master."

Again the slight dip of her chin. Then she abruptly shut her eyes tight. "But I don't," she whispered. "I like being strong. I *am* strong."

"Of course you are. And maybe that's the answer. Maybe you like *not* being strong every once in a while."

Her eyes opened again, and for the first time this morning he could see her thinking, really thinking without fear. Then she said something that was completely and totally unexpected.

"I never appreciated you in high school," she said.

"You were that nice geek. I knew you liked me, but… well, I didn't realize how rare that is."

He leaned forward onto his knees. "Rare that someone liked you?"

"Rare that someone is nice. Kind. Considerate. Helpful without pushing. Nice."

He sighed. Great. He was her lap dog. He knew that wasn't exactly what she meant. She was trying to give him a compliment, to express regret for how she'd treated him in high school. He understood that, but he wasn't interested in before. He wanted to know about now. How did she see him now? He wanted to be a man to her, not a Saint Bernard.

"Thank you for the compliment," he managed to force out. "But…" But what? He didn't know what to say, so he rubbed his hand over his face. "Look, I can't think. I haven't had any coffee, and I need a shower."

She nodded. "Coffee. Shower. Sounds like heaven." Then she flashed him a brief smile. "Especially if I get a chocolate chip scone." She bit her lip. "My treat, Jim. You shower, I'll grab breakfast. Then we can talk, okay? I promise."

He nodded, wondering if he dared trust her at her word. He gave it even odds that her fears would take over the minute she left the house. "You want to eat here or at a neutral café?"

It took her a moment to answer, but in the end, she shook her head. "Do you have a pair of sweats I could borrow?"

"Yeah. It'll be big on you, but—"

"It'll be fine. Thanks. I'll get breakfast and then come back here. I swear."

She meant it. He could see it in the stiff set to her

shoulders. So he grabbed her a set of sweats from his drawers and handed them mutely to her.

She took the clothes, her eyes huge but her expression still determined. God, she looked as if she was about to face a firing squad.

"Nicky—"

"How do you take your coffee?"

"Raspberry latte with whip," he answered, because what else could he say?

"Half hour. I promise," she said.

He touched her chin, lifting her face so that she had no choice but to look at him. He didn't know why he did it. She was already looking at him. But he needed to touch her skin, to stroke her cheek, to do everything he could to brand her with his caress.

A thousand words rushed to his mouth, all fighting to get out. But none of them were right. Nothing seemed to fit. And his body wasn't listening to his mind anyway. He swooped down and took her in a kiss. He thrust himself into her mouth, he stroked her and owned her as best as he could.

She opened to him on a gasp, but within a moment she was stretching forward, arching her back to deepen their kiss. Heaven.

But then he had to end it. "Half hour, Nicky. Or I'm going to start looking for you. I'm trying to give you space, but part of me just wants to tie you up and keep you with me forever. I'm sorry if that's too blunt, but it's the truth."

She stared at him, and her expression turned rueful. "I know. Thank you for being honest." Then she turned and ducked back into the bathroom to dress. Five minutes later, she was out the front door.

12

DARK COFFEE SPILLED out of the latte, splattering on Nicky's hand and leg. She grimaced at the dark blotch on the sweatpants—Jim's sweatpants—and tried to steady her arm, her breath, her entire life. But all three refused to cooperate, so she set down the cup on the porch rather than spill it completely.

The front door opened, and there he stood. His hair was wet, his torso gloriously naked and his jeans slung low. "Need a hand?" he asked. Then before she could answer, he came forward on bare feet to grab the latte off the porch then lift the white bag from her other hand.

He was watching her closely, and she could all but read his thoughts off his forehead. He was wondering if she was still going to skip out, find some excuse—like the ton of work she really had to get done—and disappear. Part of her wanted to. Part of her was terrified to examine the reasons behind her bizarre desires last night. But this was Jimmy Ray. He wasn't judging her. He wasn't going to hurt her. If she were going to examine the reasons behind her kinky passions with anyone, she would choose Jimmy Ray. Which meant she had to suppress her fears and walk in his front door. In a minute…

"My mug is in the car," she said, gesturing behind her. "I'm just going to grab it." She did, then quickly returned to the front stoop. Then she just stood there on his porch because he was blocking the way. "Uh, can I come in?"

He flushed a mottled red and quickly stepped aside. "Um, yeah. Sorry. I was just thinking I like the way you look in my sweats."

She grimaced. "My hair's a mess, your clothes are like two sizes too large and—"

"And I like the way you look in my sweats," he repeated.

She felt her face heat. "Um, thanks."

He held open the door for her and gestured her inside. She went in carefully, making sure she didn't touch him as she passed. But she was excruciatingly aware of his body and his breath. Jeez, even his heat seemed to envelop her, and she both loved and hated the way her skin tingled in response.

He followed a step behind her, closing the door as she moved. "The kitchen's right through—"

"I remember," she said. And she did. She remembered walking blindfolded from his television room through what was most likely his kitchen. Sure enough, the kitchen was right where she expected. What she didn't expect was the cheery yellow paint and the white appliances all drenched in sunlight from the backyard. The room was delightful.

"Nice," she said, looking all around.

"Yeah. It's the real reason I bought the house."

She turned to look at him. "I never would have guessed that."

"Guys can't like sunlight?"

"Of course they can. I just thought you would have looked at the neighborhood, evaluated the structure of the house and resale potential, balanced that with the asking price and then..."

"Made a sound investment choice?"

She nodded. "But maybe that's more me than you."

He shrugged and took a long pull on his latte. "Well, okay, so maybe I didn't realize I liked this much sun in the morning until I walked through it one bright 7:00 a.m. But I do, and I did...and this house had a huge garage and the TV room. Plus it is a good neighborhood and a good investment. So..."

"So you bought it." She nodded. "Good choice. Way better than my tiny condo downtown."

"Sounds like a good location."

She settled down at the round breakfast table. "It's a good investment," she answered honestly.

"But not a home with a big backyard and a sunlit kitchen," he said softly.

Her gaze jerked to him in surprise. He had hit it right on the head. As a single woman, she'd felt she needed to be smart about her investments, and what was a condo but an investment? Unfortunately, that had been her primary consideration, so she'd always felt like she was living in a bank account rather than in a house.

She looked away from him to gaze out at the backyard. "I forget that you're smarter than the average bear."

He settled down in a chair across from her. "Damned by faint praise."

"No," she murmured. "You're the smartest person I know. It intimidates me. You always have."

He released a snort of laughter, but immediately sobered at her look. "Sorry," he said. "It's just funny, that's all. Me intimidating you. I was scared to death every time I had to talk to you. Athlete, class president, girl most likely to—"

"Get what she wants, when she wants it, exactly how it must be for maximum yield. Yeah, I remember." She spoke the words dryly. Her high school epitaph had always haunted her.

"It's not a bad thing to know what you want," he said softly.

"What I want, how I want it," she repeated. "Sound like a self-centered bitch to you?"

He propped his chin on his hand. "Issues with high school much?"

"Says the geek who laughed when I said his intelligence was intimidating."

He sighed. "Touché."

She leaned back in her chair and looked directly at him, feeling almost as if she were back in a boardroom. It made her want to tap her pumps on the tile just to show she was in control. It was a lie, of course. She was way out of control, but she allowed herself two taps on the floor. One. Two.

"So to summarize," she said in her most impressive tone. "Here's what I'm afraid of. You're the high school geek who always wanted to do the class president. You see me as the high school queen bee who needed to be taken down a peg. Mission accomplished. You've done me. I'm embarrassed." Her cheeks flushed hot, but she kept doggedly on. "Do you check off this and move on to the rest of your life?"

He leaned back in his chair, folded his arms across his chest and tapped his foot twice. In short, he echoed everything she'd just done, only he added an arch of his eyebrow. Without saying a word, he showed her exactly how *not* intimidated he was.

She flushed hotter and looked away.

"Here's what I'm afraid of. Something scared you, some time in your life. Maybe some guy, I don't know. But it was big enough that you suppressed everything that makes you passionate and whole. You've spent all your life since climbing the corporate ladder but it's making you nuts."

She shivered, knowing everything he said was true though not exactly in the way he thought. "Why does that scare you?" she asked when she could finally find her voice.

"Because I don't know when your fears are going to overwhelm you and you'll bolt." He reached across the table to touch her hand. "I don't want you to bolt. I had a great time last night, and I thought you did, too."

She had. She did. And worse, she couldn't stop herself from wanting to do it again. But the mortification of it all, this terrible morning after… It just wasn't worth it. Or so she kept telling herself.

"So what happened, Nicky? What happened to the girl you used to be?"

"The girl most likely to run the country in twenty years?"

He nodded. "Yeah. Her."

She shrugged, wondering if she could explain. "Life happened. Life isn't high school. I thought it would be so easy, but then I couldn't get a good job out of college. So I borrowed a ton of money and went to graduate school, which was harder than I ever thought possible. And then

I had to get a job to pay all that debt. I work harder and harder, but the goal keeps slipping further away."

"And what's that goal?"

She played with the texture of her disposable cup, rubbing her thumb up and down the smooth paper. Below the table, her left hand was gripping her thigh so tight, she was sure she was giving herself bruises.

"I don't know. Success. Happiness. The usual."

He was silent for a long time, just watching her rub the edge of the cup. He took another pull from his latte. So did she. And then, finally, he spoke. "Let's go on a date. A simple, get-to-know-you-better date."

She arched a brow at him. "You sure you're not looking for a sequel of last night?" It was a throwaway question. He was a guy, after all. But he also wanted the normal date stuff. She knew he was sincere in what he said. She just didn't know how she felt about it.

Surprisingly enough, he didn't answer with an equally throwaway response. His eyes grew troubled. "I'm still processing last night," he finally said. "I...uh...I don't know that I can top it."

She blinked. "Performance fears?"

He released a short laugh. "You're a whole lot of woman, Nicky. Any man who isn't a little bit anxious is just deluding himself."

She stared at him, seeing the slight flush in his cheeks until he ducked his head down to drink his latte. Then she started to laugh. A real, deep down belly laugh. She had no idea why she thought this was funny, but the more she tried to speak, the more funny it became. Oh god, it felt good to laugh.

It took a moment for her to stop laughing. Long moments when he watched her, his cheeks bright red, but his eyes slowly lightening with humor. In the end, she finally was able to gasp out an explanation of sorts.

"I guess I'm not the only one still stuck in high school, huh?" She took another breath to steady her nerves. "You sit there bare chested, showing off your sculpted abs. You live in a house four times the size of my condo, have a net worth well beyond anything I could earn in a decade, and just gave me the fantasy night of the millennium. I think you can dispense with the I'm-a-clueless-geek persona. Nobody's buying it, least of all me."

He leaned forward, his expression fierce. "So I'm not the only smart one in the room."

She smiled, but the tension in her belly coiled even higher. He wanted to see her on a different level—a *personal* level—and that scared her. "I gave up on men a long time ago, Jimmy. I...uh...made some bad choices in grad school."

His eyes darkened. "Were you hurt?"

She shook her head. "Not physically. Emotionally wrecked." And financially, but she wasn't ready to confess that. No way was she going to admit that her boyfriend, the man she thought she was going to marry, had taken her for every dime she had. "I'm just afraid to try again."

"I get that," he said softly. "I've dated a few really bad choices. Nothing seriously, though, because I've spent my adult life working nonstop. Or hiding in my garage." He shrugged. "Girls terrified me in high school and were too time-consuming in adulthood." He leaned forward. "But you're worth the effort, Nicky. You're worth the risk."

She swallowed, stunned by how his statement slid down her spine right into her soul. He made her feel so damned special. But she was still afraid. And still crazy busy at work. "I'm just not sure this is a good time," she hedged.

He touched her hand. A light stroke, but she felt it as if he'd touched her entire body. Which, of course, he had last night. "Mindless sex with you is great, Nicky. It's beyond great. But I want more from you. Are you woman enough to give it to me?"

"You challenging me?" she asked, her brow arched.

"Will that get you to say yes?" he shot back.

She bit her lip. Could she do it? Could she take the risk on him? It was so hard to do. What if he got to know her and realized she was just a midlevel manager with midlevel intelligence?

"Nicky," he huffed. "It's not acquisitions and mergers. It's just a date."

She shook her head, the words coming out without thought. "I like Jimmy. I like what I remember of him. He was safe and funny and he liked me. I don't want to lose him."

"Jimmy's still here. But I'm more than just Jimmy. I'm a grown man. Don't you think you deserve a grown-up?"

And if the grown-up didn't like the woman? The real woman? The question pounded in her head, the insecurity gripping her like a vise. "The last time I felt successful, felt like I could handle anything, was back in high school. After that…" She winced. "Well, after that I discovered that the real world is way harder than I ever imagined."

"You're up to it, Nicky."

She wasn't sure. It was ridiculous. She was an accomplished woman, successful at her job, had the respect of her peers. And yet she was still a mass of insecurities.

He touched her cheek. His thumb caressed a long stroke down her jaw line, then he gripped her chin, drawing her forward. She didn't go far. He was the one who leaned across the table to stroke his mouth over hers. He teased the seam of her lips, then pushed inside the moment she relaxed.

Bit by bit her insecurities faded to nothing. The play of his tongue brushed them away as well as good portions of her will. In this arena, he was powerful beyond belief, and she willingly surrendered to him.

Within moments, she was arching toward him and wrapping her hand around his head. If he wanted it, she would lie down right there and let him slide right in.

"Nicky," he rasped as he broke the kiss. "Nicky, just say yes."

"Yes," she answered.

He stroked his tongue along her neck, and she purred in response. "Yes to sex? Or yes to a date?"

"Just yes," she said.

He shifted his hands so that they cupped the back of her head and pulled back to look into her eyes. "Nicky…"

"Is there a condom in your pocket?" she asked.

He nodded.

"Once more," she said. "One more mindless sex encounter right here, right now. And then tomorrow, we'll meet like dates. We'll do the awkward who are you, what have you been doing since high school, stupid date thing. But for right now…" She was already reaching to unzip his jeans.

"Deal," he said.

It took him a moment. There was awkward fumbling

for them both. But within a minute, she was settled on top of his kitchen table, and he was stepping between her thighs. He slid in slowly, a groan of delight on his lips.

At his urging, she wrapped her legs around him then arched her back, planting her palms behind her for support. That gave him full access to her breasts, which he stroked and manipulated just as she liked.

God, he was big. She liked the way he stretched her all the way to her spine. She liked that he was so thick that she felt every ridge during his slow withdrawal and abrupt thrust. The one thing that she didn't like was that he looked at her. His eyes held her gaze as he thrust into her. No matter what his hands did, no matter that the table was moving in time to his beat, no matter that he slipped his thumb between them and brought her quickly to a writhing scream. He held her gaze during the whole thing. He held her. He saw her.

Then he abruptly gripped her hips and slammed hard into her. She thought he would close his eyes and shudder as all men did, but he didn't. He still held her gaze and she thought he might have even whispered her name.

Either way, they reached their peaks staring eye to eye with one another. It added a whole new dimension that was both terrifying and exciting. His eyes, his expression, his entire presence seemed to fill her head with him, just him. So much so that his orgasm triggered another for her. And then one more until she had to look away because it was too much.

Too much pleasure. Too much intimacy.

She felt him lean forward, his chest still heaving as he gasped for air. She was too weak to support him, but he didn't collapse on top of her. He just let his forehead drop against hers as they both recovered.

"I'll pick you up at seven," he said. She smelled raspberry and coffee on his breath, and inhaled just to experience it again.

"You want more?" she asked. Wasn't he afraid? Didn't he know she was already at her limit?

"Everything, Nicky. I want to know everything about you."

It might have sounded creepy, but she shivered in excitement. More. He wanted more of her.

"Don't you?" he asked.

Yes. No. "Yes," she whispered. He made her feel brave enough to do anything. Or perhaps when she was so filled with him, she couldn't think of her fears. She barely thought at all.

"Wear something nice," he said. He had recovered enough that he was beginning to kiss her face. Her nose first, then her cheeks. Finally her lips.

She answered in kind, and she felt his cock pulse deep inside her. She smiled and tightened her internal muscles. He groaned in response.

"All woman," he said against her lips. "I don't know that I can keep up."

This time she was the one who sought his eyes, who touched his cheek until she got his entire attention. "The moment you stop, I'll run."

He blinked. "Why?"

"I just do. I'll start thinking and then I'm out the door." She sighed. "Work to do. A portfolio to build."

He took a deep breath. His chest expanded against hers, his heat enveloped her, and his arms came around to support her from behind. He surrounded her and his grip kept tightening. He pulled her against him until she was nearly crushed. But she didn't fight him. She loved it.

"You're not going anywhere," he said.

"Okay," she returned. When he said it like that, she agreed without thought.

But then her watch beeped. She had work to do, reports to compile, layoffs to avoid. He grunted in disgust, but then his phone rang and so he sighed and pulled himself out of her.

She let him go. She had no choice what with her own work intruding. Ten minutes later, she was dressed again and he was cursing into his phone. She was heading for the door when he dropped his cell to his chest.

"Seven o'clock," he said. "Wear something nice."

She nodded. Then she shook her head. "Tomorrow night. I can't tonight."

He grimaced, but then they both heard someone calling to him from the other end of his cell. He winced. "Fine. Tomorrow night."

She smiled and opened his front door.

"I mean it, Nicky. I'm not letting you change your mind."

"Of course not," she answered blithely, but they both knew she was halfway out the door—both literally and figuratively. He wanted too much from her. She didn't have—

He grabbed hold of her arm. She didn't even know he'd moved, but he was there, whipping her around to face him.

"Do you know what the difference is between Jimmy and Jim?"

She shook her head. Her heart was beating so hard in her throat she didn't think she could get a word out.

"Jimmy wanted you from the first day of freshman

year, but he didn't have the balls to go for it. To go for you."

She looked at him, her eyes narrowing as she saw the strength in the man that was never in the boy. "And Jim?" she prompted.

"Jim will pick you up tomorrow at seven. Jim isn't giving up without a fight."

The resolve in his words sizzled over her skin. It promised things to her on a subconscious level. It told her that he was a man of his word. He would find her. He would claim her. And it would be the most amazing ride of her life.

God, she wanted that. Yes, she wanted him to claim her, but she also wanted his absolute confidence. For him, just saying something made it true. Maybe that was why he was such a good hypnotist. There was power in his voice, and if he said something, the universe scrambled to comply.

"Jim better be sure he knows what he wants," she returned. If he got her to open up to him, then changed his mind, it would kill her. If she gave him her time and her heart and he found her not worthy, she doubted she would recover. She didn't have the strength for that on top of everything else.

"You're safe with me," he said softly.

Was she? When he said it like that, she almost believed him. "Guess we'll find out tomorrow."

"Guess so." He stood in the doorway and watched her all the way down the street.

13

JIM STOOD at Nicky's condo door and listened intently. She was home, thank God. It was Sunday night and time for their date. His first fear had been that she wouldn't even be there when he showed up. But she was. She even opened the door within moments of his knock. He felt the tension in his shoulders release, but that was all that eased up beneath his black tux. The rest of him was rock hard and straining forward since Nicky looked like a wet dream come to life. She wore a black dress with an interesting diamond-shaped cutout between throat and cleavage. Her skirt was tight and short above legs that stretched down to black stilettos. And if he wasn't mistaken, she was wearing black stockings with a seam up the back. Gold bracelets jingled from her left wrist as she waved him inside, but that was the only welcoming sound he heard.

"I know it's Sunday night!" she snapped. She shoved a decorative gold comb into her hair with enough force to pierce bone. "And if you'd done the spreadsheet right on Friday, then you wouldn't be losing your Sunday Night Football time now." She frowned. "What? I don't care what sport you're missing! Go do the report tonight or you're fired!"

Then she ripped a Bluetooth attachment out of her ear and whipped it across the room in fury. Jim watched it bounce twice on the couch cushions before hopping the armrest and landing on the floor.

"Basketball," he said to her bare back. "Big playoff tonight."

"Yeah. He said that," she snapped. Then she took a deep breath, obviously trying to steady her emotions. "This is all your fault, you know," she said with a small touch of humor.

"Really?" he drawled. "How so?"

"I didn't figure out that the moron had done the wrong report until this afternoon. If I'd had my head on straight Friday, I would have realized it then, told him to fix it before he left for the weekend, and then he'd be right now sitting down for chips and dip in front of his flat-screen."

He leaned against the door jamb and slipped the clear package he was carrying onto an entryway table. He hadn't even fully entered the condo, but with her in this mood he wasn't sure it was safe to progress. So he stayed where he was and waited for her attention.

Eventually he was rewarded when she turned back to him, a single eyebrow arched. "Don't you want to know why my mistake is your fault?"

"It sounds like it was moron's mistake, but go ahead. Why is it my fault?"

She folded her arms, mimicking his pose. Except that when she did it, her breasts rose and her cleavage deepened. "It's your fault because I've had a bitch of a time working these last few days. Because of you."

He smiled. "Am I supposed to feel guilty about that?"

"Yes. Terribly guilty. So guilty you intend to rock my world during tonight's date to make up for it." Then she winked at him, her lips curving into a wicked smile.

She was teasing him, he realized, and he grinned. "One world-rocking date coming up," he returned, praying that it was true.

She nodded, then gestured to his cell phone, which it was clipped to his black cummerbund. "What about you? Get that techno-engineering thing worked out?"

"Software patch working so far," he said. They might not have seen each other since Saturday morning, but they'd been e-mailing work woes back and forth all weekend. "But the problem is complicated. It's going to take a lot of time to work out. They want to hire me on full-time until I get it sorted out."

She tilted her head. "Are you going to do it?"

He shook his head. "I doubt it. I've already e-mailed them the solution to the biggest problem. The rest is—" he waved his hand "—details."

"That's where the devil resides," she drawled.

"So I hear."

She tilted her head, studying him. "But you're not going to do it. Not paying you enough?"

"No. They're offering plenty." He shrugged. "I don't know. I've done the workday grind. And this is going to be a big grind. I'm just…"

"Happy being an amateur magician in your brother's club?"

He shrugged. "Not really. I don't know. Professionally, I'm wandering right now. Looking for inspiration." Then he conspicuously looked her up and down…slowly. God, she was gorgeous.

"Somehow I don't think that's the kind of inspiration required," she drawled, but her voice had turned sultry and her eyes were languid. His blood slipped straight south as her nipples became clearly outlined by the otherwise smooth black fabric of her dress.

In the end, she broke first, sliding her eyes away as she turned toward her kitchen. "Do you want a drink or something? I've got wine and a variety of hard liquors. Get whatever you like." There was a tasteful display of alcoholic options on a cabinet especially designed for the purpose. "And while you're pouring, you can tell me if I need to change into a gown to match your tux."

"No need. You look great." He grabbed the plastic box off the table and presented her with a wrist corsage. "This is for you." Odd how his heart was beating triple time at this. It was just a stupid flower, and yet…

Her eyes lit up when she saw it. Two pink roses intertwined with gold ribbon and green stuff. "It's beautiful. Wow, thank you!" She opened the box reverently, stroking the petals as she looked up at him. "No one's given me a corsage since high school."

"Then it's about time." He lifted it out of the box and held open the elastic strap for her to slip her hand inside. It felt weirdly like putting a wedding ring on her, and he surprised himself by how right it felt. Then he had a moment's panic at the bizarre turn his brain had taken.

Nicky raised her wrist to smell the flowers, then peered at him over the floral display. "This isn't feeling like a usual date."

He smiled, though the movement was awkward. He was still reeling from having to force his thoughts away from weddings. "You asked for a rock-my-world date."

"So I did. But I was only teasing—" Her phone rang, and she stifled a curse. Her eyes immediately started scanning the couch for her earpiece. He was debating whether to point to the item where it had rolled beneath an end table when she stomped into her bedroom. There was more cursing as she presumably spoke to whomever it was after locating her cell in there.

That, naturally, gave him time to inspect her surroundings in better detail. Like him, she had a flat-screen TV, high-end speaker system and DVR. But the remotes were set neatly on top of the wet bar, far away from both television and couch. That told him that though she had the equipment, she didn't watch. He already knew she wasn't a heavy drinker, so all of it—electronics, alcohol, the sleek furniture—was for guests.

Stepping deeper into the room, he glanced at the three rooms off the main space: bedroom, bathroom, office. The bedroom door was shut, so no information there. The bathroom was like the kitchen: pristine and obviously for guests. The office, though, was exactly what he expected.

Nicky lived in that room. It was overflowing with files, up-to-date computer equipment and an avalanche of papers. He saw an empty coffee mug, half-filled water bottle and an untouched scone.

"So you found my disaster area. Think I should call Hazmat?"

He turned to her with a guilty start. "Sorry. I guess I was prying."

She shrugged. "That, too, is par for the course on first dates." Then she pulled a velvet-and-lace black shawl around her shoulders, its delicate femininity somehow enhancing the sleek lines of her dress. "I'm ready to go."

"Your Bluetooth earpiece is under that end table," he said as he pointed.

"So it is." She looked, but didn't move.

"Did you want me to get it for you?"

She grinned. "Nope. I've declared this a real date. No phone. No Bluetooth. No office calls at all. I even changed my voice mail to say that I'm off duty until Monday morning."

He smiled, feeling very pleased. "So I've got you to myself for thirteen whole hours. My, the possibilities are endless."

"Yes," she said with a wink. "They are." And off she went in those stiletto heels, pulling open the door with a style that was all Nicky. Sexy Nicky, not corporate raider Nicky.

Jim couldn't suppress his grin. No matter what, this was going to be one hell of a night.

14

"WE'RE EATING HERE?" Nicky gasped, her tone conveying only half her disbelief. "A greasy spoon?"

He shook his head. "Not *a* greasy spoon. *The* greasy spoon. Don't you remember?"

She frowned out the broad windshield of his Corvette, thinking hard. One by one the pieces fell into place. First there was the tux, then the corsage. Next came this car with the engine he'd rebuilt. Course, back then it had been a Chevy, but the concept was the same. And now they were pulling into very same "restaurant" they had gone to after her ill-fated senior prom.

"You're reliving high school," she said, equal parts charmed and appalled.

"Sort of," he said as he leaned forward in the seat to look directly at her. "Look, I'm happy to take you to the best restaurant in town. I can afford it and you more than deserve it."

"But…" she prompted when he fell silent.

"But this is where our story should have started. I should have asked you to prom, rented a tux and taken you to…well, a better restaurant—"

"But this is what we did. So you're re-creating that night with minor alterations. Why?"

"Because there were things I should have asked you back then. Things I should have done. Look, I'm not trying to go back in time. I'm just trying to reframe our story now." He flushed slightly and looked out toward the diner's neon Open sign. "I guess it was a bad idea."

"No," she said slowly. "It's unusual, but I'm willing to go with it. But if you start wanting to dance to the Backstreet Boys, I'm outta here."

"No Backstreet Boys. I swear." Then he pushed open the door and rushed around the car.

She was more than capable of opening her own door, but in this tight skirt she was grateful that he gave her a hand stepping out. And charmed that he did it with elegant machismo.

"You are very handsome in that tux, Mr. Ray."

"I borrowed it from the Magic Man."

She glanced shyly at him, feeling a little outclassed. "Genius engineer, performing magician/hypnotist and restorer of classic cars. Anything else about you that I should know?"

He pretended to think about it. "Good in bed?"

"I can't speak to that. I don't think we've ever done it in an actual bed." Then she laughed at his abrupt frown. But he didn't say anything, since they were walking into the diner.

The waitress, fry cook and two cops did a double take when they entered. All four were grinning by the time he handed her into the booth. A bubble of laughter worked its way up her chest, but she didn't release it. She was happy to hold it inside, feeling an absurd amount of joy at the situation. And when she looked at his eyes across the table, she saw an answering delight there. The waitress greeted them and offered them menus, but Nicky just shook her head. She'd bet anything that Jim knew just what she wanted.

He did. "Two double cheeseburgers and sundaes for dessert. Pistachio ice cream."

Nicky grinned. "You got it in one." Then she opened her paper napkin and set it carefully in her lap. But before long, the silence needed something: questions, answers, first-date stuff. But who was going to start first?

She looked up and found him watching her intently. She flushed, slightly embarrassed by his intense stare. "You've known me for years," she finally said. "What could you possibly find so fascinating about me?"

"You mean besides beauty, discipline and excellence…um, out of bed."

She arched a brow. If this was going to descend into the back and forth of sexual innuendo, she was going to rapidly tire of the conversation. She already knew they had chemistry on that level. She'd thought this date was about finding what else they had in common.

Fortunately, he was a step ahead of her. He leaned back in the booth and smiled. "So tell me about college. Where'd you go, what was your major—"

"The personal résumé," she said, nodding. "You looking for the whole schpiel, including ex-boyfriends?"

He shuddered. "God, no. I'm already jealous of the men who touched the virgin goddess, and I made them up. Just give me the path from high school to executive."

She took a moment to answer. It wasn't what he was asking that threw her. It was his offhand comment about jealousy. He was a multimillionaire, for God's sake.

And he was jealous of men—made-up men—who had touched her?

A shiver of delight skated down her spine. She knew it wasn't PC of her, but she liked his flash of possessiveness. So she rewarded him with a warm smile and an "accidental" brush of her foot against his calf. His eyes shot wide, but she had already shifted away. Let him wonder if she'd done it on purpose or not.

"It's really not that exciting," she began. So she told the whole story in more detail than she'd given him before. Yes, she'd gotten her degree, but college had been a lot tougher than high school. College work was harder than high school. Getting a job out of college was even harder. And clawing her way into management had taken an MBA and some serious sweat. She wasn't a natural genius like he was. She'd had to work damn hard to get where she was now, and she was proud of her accomplishments. "But I just can't shake the feeling that I'm about to be found out," she confessed between bites of cheeseburger.

"Found out? About what?"

"Any minute now, someone younger and smarter is going to point out just how many mistakes I've made along the way. I've missed things. I'm human. All it takes is one smarty-pants, and then I'll be out on my ear."

He frowned. "Smarty-pants?"

"Yeah, you know. Someone who understood high school physics without cracking a book. Someone who likes retooling engines in his spare time and who put together a brilliant idea and sold it for millions before he was twenty-seven."

"You mean me," he said dully.

"Yes, you." Then she stole a French fry off his plate.

"Well, no, not you specifically. I don't think you're planning on applying for my job anytime soon."

"God, no—"

"But someone like you. Someone with better ideas, a better education, a better *brain*." She bit down harder than she intended on his French fry. She hadn't intended to expose quite so much of her psyche to him. This certainly wasn't a first-date topic, but that was the beauty of time spent with Jim. They had so much history together even with the ten-year lag. She trusted him. And given that trust, way too much of her inner life spilled out from her mouth.

So she chomped on French fries rather than say more. And he sipped his soda, his prodigious mind obviously churning. She was almost afraid to ask what he was thinking. She didn't want to hear him say something like, you're right. You're a moron and I don't want anything more to do with you.

Fortunately, she was spared that humiliation with the arrival of their sundaes. Less fortunately, he wasn't a man to let things slide. Once the ice cream had been appropriately served, sampled and "mmmmm"-ed over, he set down his spoon and took a deep breath.

"I think I'm seeing a pattern here."

She arched a brow. "Don't read too much into things here. I'm—"

"Just hear me out. You're afraid that someone with better credentials is going to oust you from your job. That your boss is going to throw you over the minute someone with a better résumé comes along."

Her shoulders tightened because, yes, he had just voiced her greatest fear. So rather than speak, she toyed with the chocolate as it dripped from her spoon.

"If I'd worked up the nerve to ask you out for prom, would you have accepted?"

She looked up from her ice cream to blink at him. "That was an abrupt change in topic."

"Yes, it was, but answer the question. Would you have accepted?"

She looked away. "No, probably not," she confessed.

"Right. Because I was a geek, he was head of the wrestling team. In high school terms, he had better credentials than I did."

She winced. Wow, did that make her sound shallow or what? "I don't think that way anymore, Jim. I think you're great."

"Only because you're looking at different credentials now. I'm smart, a millionaire, and I went to MIT. Good credentials."

She huffed and set down her spoon. "That's not how I judge you. You're also a great guy, you make me feel safe and..." And the sex had been great.

He grinned, obviously guessing where her thoughts were going. "Okay, so you've grown. I've grown. In high school, you were just the smart volleyball star that I worshiped from afar. I never really saw how determined you are, how strong you can be and yet how..."

"I still have a submissive sex kitten side. Yeah, I know." Her face heated as she said it. She still wasn't quite sure what to make of her own fantasies, but then again that was the beauty of fantasies. They weren't you. They were pretend.

"My point is that you're so much more than your credentials, Nicky. Your boss has got to see that, too. You don't have anything to fear."

She arched a brow. "You assume more intelligence in upper management than I do."

He shook his head. "You see too little of yourself. Trust me. Everyone else sees more of you than your résumé and your mistakes."

She looked back at her sundae, wanting to believe what he said. But the truth was so much smaller than what he suggested.

"The truth is," she said slowly, "that you're the only one who sees that. Who sees me."

"Believe me, Nicky, everyone sees you on your cell phone. Everyone knows you work weekends and nights."

"But you're the one who asked about my fantasies. You're the only one who knows my fears, too, about being passed over or thrown out because I'm not good enough."

He leaned forward. "But you are good enough. You're ten thousand times good enough. You're the only one who doesn't believe it."

She looked him in the eyes, saw the absolute sincerity in there, and knew he believed what he said with total conviction. He saw more than her lackluster college degree and slightly above-average brain. He saw her work, her dedication, and her willingness to go the extra ten miles. And, of course, he'd seen the other side—the skanky side—and hadn't been repulsed.

Which made him one in a million. More like one in a billion because when he said it, she believed it. She saw herself as competent and valuable, too. Her fears eased, her faith in herself grew.

"You're a pretty special guy," she said softly.

"I'm trying hard to live up to your standard," he returned.

She smiled, her heart melting with his words. She so wanted to jump him right then. But she also was desperate just to spend more time talking with him, learning what he thought, what made him tick.

So she consciously reined in her libido and took a big bite of ice cream to cool her internal jets. It didn't work, but it helped. And when she finished swallowing, she was able to look back at him.

"It's your turn now. I want to know everything you've been doing since high school."

"Well, there was college, then career, blah-blah. And then a couple nights ago, I reconnected with the hottest woman I've ever known. And get this…" He leaned forward. "She lets me act out fantasies with her."

"Hmmm. Sounds kinky."

"And weirdly liberating."

She raised her eyebrows, inviting him to continue.

"I can pay the bill. We can go back to my place—"

She raised her hand, cutting off his words. "This is a first date, remember? I don't go home with just anybody. So start talking, and no blah-blah this time."

He tilted his head. "Isn't that the first rule of dating—don't talk about yourself?"

"Not tonight, it isn't. Really, Jim, I want to know more about you. Where have you lived? What do you do for fun? Everything."

"Seriously?"

"Seriously." And she meant it. With every fiber of her being. "And then afterward, we can see about those kinky fantasies." She leaned forward onto her arms. "How did you start hypnotizing people?"

He shrugged. "Shy kid. Too many comic books. If I could figure out how to hypnotize people, I could have whatever I wanted, including hot girls. Trust me when I say I'm not the only boy with that particular fantasy."

"But you're the only one I know who succeeded. Girl and all." She propped her chin on her hand. "I never would have pegged you for a stage act."

He laughed, the sound coming out a little tight and self-conscious. "I got good at magic when I was eight. Spent hours in my room practicing, but I never showed anyone except my brother, Rick. Even my parents were too much of a risk."

She frowned. "Oh, come on. Your parents? No one is that shy."

"I was. My dad thought it was all a stupid waste of time and said so often. My mom agreed with whatever my dad said."

She winced. "That must have been really hard."

He toyed with the whipped cream on his sundae. "It wasn't all bad. I had a good home, good food, all the basics. Dad taught me about electricity which led to robotics and engineering. That got me into MIT on scholarship."

"Which eventually led to your million-dollar idea. But truthfully, what about the hypnotism? The stage act? I can't seem to make that fit the picture."

His sundae had turned into a soupy mess, so he set his spoon aside. "That's because you don't realize how much a CEO has to speak in public, sell his ideas to investors and the like. Think about your job. How many times do you speak to a crowd?"

She did it every week. Not to groups of hundreds or anything, but there were always reports to the higher-ups, motivational words for her subordinates, the regular ebb and flow of communication in a corporate structure. E-mail was one thing, but she often had to pitch her ideas to her boss, then sell it again to her subordinates. "But that's not the same thing as being onstage."

"Very true. But I was really shy. Choke on my tongue, coffee on my lap, falling on my face shy. When the words mattered, I could always be counted on to be throwing up in the bathroom."

She laughed at his joke, but she could also see he was dead serious. "I don't remember you being that bad in high school."

"That's because I made sure to never say anything important to anyone. The most I did was ask questions. A lot of questions."

She nodded. She absolutely remembered that. "You asked good questions. And you listened to the answer." Jimmy had always been a good listener.

He nodded. "But once I had this company, I couldn't spend meetings throwing up in the bathroom."

"You could have hired a speaker, a professional marketer."

He shook his head. "Not in the early days. I didn't have the money. My mom suggested hypnotherapy."

"You saw a hypnotist?"

He laughed. "Didn't have the money."

Oh my god. She got it. She knew exactly what he did. "You bought a book on hypnotism and tried to do it yourself."

He nodded. "It's what geeks do. They read. They study. They learn to do for themselves."

"Did it work? Were you able to mesmerize yourself?"

He shook his head. "Not in the least. In the end it was Rick who gave me the answer."

She waited, her own sundae forgotten. "Well?"

"He'd bought his club by then, but it was struggling.

Amateur night was a good draw, but he didn't have enough acts. So he begged me to fill in. Said if I could go onstage and make someone quack like a duck, then I could face down a boardroom no problem."

"And that convinced you?"

"Hell, no. But he's my brother. He really needed some help. Plus he offered to pay me half the night's profit."

She snorted. "Was there any that night?"

"No, but it didn't matter. He's my brother. I'd tried everything else, and frankly, I could hardly be worse than the rest of the acts."

She could well believe that. "So you did it. You just went onstage and did it."

"Well, it took a few vodkas to get me up there the first night, but yeah, I did it. And it worked. I survived. I even got better onstage." He took a big spoonful of his ice cream soup. "I don't know if you remember, but I'm not that great onstage. I don't have the charisma or showmanship that's needed for a great stage act."

She frowned. She remembered thinking he looked cute in his tux, but she didn't remember him being especially funny or entertaining. Not until he dropped into his sexy voice and her mind found the way to turn off. "I thought you did fine."

"Fine for a bar act. And only when someone cancels on short notice and Rick is desperate."

"But—" she began. He cut her off.

"It worked, Nicky. I got over my fears, and better yet, I happened to be subbing in when an old high school fantasy walked in."

She shook her head. She didn't know whether to admire his determination to face his fear or be envious that even crippling shyness faded away under the force of his will. Both, she supposed. He was really smart and really determined. Good things happened to people who had that combination.

"So," she said, "you got over your fear."

He nodded. "Which made a real difference when it came time to sell my company. And now I dabble." He shrugged. "I play with stuff in my garage hoping for my next great idea. And as long as I'm confessing fears, let me tell you that I'm terrified I've already shot my wad, so to speak."

She frowned. "Um…I don't get it."

"I've been brilliant. I've made my fortune. Maybe I've used up all my good ideas."

She blinked. "You're not serious, are you? I mean, think about what we did a few nights ago. Believe me—"

He flushed. "Those ideas aren't hard to come by. But brilliant engineering concepts? I don't know."

"Maybe you just haven't really tried. I mean, why would you? You've got everything you need."

He shook his head. "It's not about need. It's about…I don't know. Inspiration? Luck? Maybe I've used mine all up."

"You haven't. I'm sure of it."

He looked at her. Then a moment later, he huffed and looked down. "Sorry. I can't think engineering when you're across from me. I keep thinking about your legs. And that black seam."

She laughed, really laughed. The sound was light, and she realized her chest didn't feel so tight. She wasn't hypnotized and yet she could breathe. "Well, perhaps you're just getting a different type of inspiration."

"How soon can we go home?"

She leaned back, liking their byplay. Despite his words, she didn't feel pressure to just leap into the car and head to his sex lair. And when he mimicked her relaxed pose, she knew she'd read him right. "Soon," she finally answered. "But not too soon."

"Vague, imprecise words. Yeah, that's just what we engineers love not." But then he gestured to the waitress and ordered them both coffee and another sundae to share. Hot fudge this time.

15

"CAN I SEE YOUR GARAGE?" she asked.

Jim felt a surge of lust course through him, but he kept his expression smooth. They were just now heading home at midnight. After hours of talk at the diner, he'd driven over to their old high school just to see it. Since it was such a nice night, they ended up walking around, talking some more, and even holding hands.

Bizarrely enough, that was the most amazing part of the night. They were so at ease with one another that holding hands had seemed completely natural. When had that ever happened? Most of his dates either got bored or manipulative. Or were dumb as rocks. He'd dated a ton of rocks.

Actually, that wasn't totally true. Most of the women he knew had brains, they just didn't bother to use them. Nicky did. And she was always striving to learn more. That put her at Einstein level in his book.

"Earth to Jimmy! Come in, Jimmy!"

"Jim," he responded automatically. "And I'm afraid that garage question sent all my blood away from my brain."

"I just want to see it. Without the blindfold."

"Oh. Okay." He tried to hide his disappointment, but apparently failed. Nicky burst out laughing.

"It's Sunday night! I've got to work in the morning. Did you really expect fantasy bondage play tonight?"

He glanced sideways. "Expect? Never. Hope…"

"I don't do that on first dates," she said primly.

She said it so firmly that he believed her. But then he saw the twinkle in her eye and the way her nipples were tight and hard, and his dick stiffened to the point of pain. Circumstances might prevent them from having more fun tonight, but she was certainly thinking about it.

"Whatever works for you," he said. "I'm good either way."

She laughed. "Liar. But thanks."

"No, seriously." He slowed the car at a traffic light and took the moment to touch her hand. "Tonight has been fabulous. I don't think I've talked this much with a woman ever. I'm good with—"

She kissed him. Full on the mouth, tongue and everything. It was all he could do not to climb over the stick and take her right there. They didn't pull apart until someone honked behind them.

"Um, right," he said as he put the car in gear. "Um."

"Your house. Garage," she said.

"But, uh…work tomorrow. Late night. I don't…um…" Crap, it was hard to think.

"It's okay, Jim. Take me to your garage." She intoned it like "Take me to your leader," and he had to glance sideways at her for a clue as to what exactly she was thinking.

Bad move. Very bad move. Her cheeks were flushed,

her nipples were hard, and one shoulder of her dress had slipped down to reveal the curve of her breast and the fact that all he had to do was reach out one finger to slip it beneath the fabric and stroke a tight nipple.

"I am going to do you so hard," he said without even realizing. Then the words penetrated his clouded mind and he nearly choked. Oh god, had he just said that aloud?

"Really?" she drawled, obviously enjoying the sexual byplay. "What if I don't want to be done?"

Keep your eyes on the road! You can't have sex if you crash!

"Then tell me now, because right now I want to handcuff you to a table, bend you over and thrust my dick into you so hard you'll feel like you're giving me a blow job."

She choked on her laughter at that image, and he flushed. Yeah, that was rather crude.

"I suppose that's one way of avoiding teeth," she said sweetly. "But maybe I won't wait. Maybe I'll just slip off my dress right here and do myself while you're forced to drive."

"What?" he gasped. Fortunately, when he finally stopped at a red light and could look at her, she was sitting there prim as could be. "Don't tease me like that," he said.

She didn't smile. Instead, she narrowed her eyes in thought. "Just how good a hypnotist are you?"

He shook his head. "Not that good, actually. You're the best subject I've ever had."

"Hmmm," she said. "Do it now. Hypnotize me right here, right now."

"Nicky, we're at a red light."

She pulled his face to hers. "Just try. Just drop into

that mesmerizing voice and tell me to trust you. Tell me
I'm safe."

He smiled at her. "Nicky, you *are* safe with me. You
know that." He didn't consciously drop into his mesmerizing voice, as she put it. He didn't do anything but try
to project that he was sincere. She was safe with him.
But the moment he said it, he saw the change in her. Her
eyes grew soft, her expression became more seductive
as she moistened her lips.

"Nicky?"

"Click," she purred. Then she took a deep breath,
stretching her hands high and back as far as they could
go in his Corvette. Which wasn't far, but it was far
enough for him to see the outline of her breasts full
and pointed. "You're good," she continued. "I'm right
here on my happy island of pleasure."

He was pretty sure that he'd had nothing to do with
it. If she was hypnotized, she'd done it to herself. He'd
merely provided the excuse. Fortunately, the light
turned green. "Just relax, Nicky. I'll have you home in
a moment."

"I am relaxed," she murmured. "And I believe we
were talking about you doing me hard in your garage,
but that I don't want to wait."

"Just a few more minutes—"

"Ummmm, that feels good."

He glanced over at her. Holy crap, she was indeed
slipping her dress off her shoulders to tease her nipples.
Just as she had threatened doing a minute ago!

"Keep your eyes on the road, Jimmy," she said. "You
promised to keep me safe." Then she planted her stiletto
heels up on his dash. He would have objected, except
her tight skirt slid all the way up.

Oh my god, she wasn't wearing any underwear!

"Nicky, you're taking your life into your hands. I'm still a guy driving a car. I need some blood in my brain."

"Ooooooh. I get a shiver right at the base of my neck when someone starts stroking my clit."

Sweet heaven, while one hand was thumbing her nipple, the other was between her legs presumably doing exactly what...

He could smell her. Her musk was thick in the air and his brain was fading beneath the lust. "Nicky..." he ground out. "I never knew you to be a sadist."

"You tie me up, I tie you up. Just in a different way. Stop sign."

"What—shi—!" He slammed on the brakes, jerking them both forward. Thankfully there was no one behind him, but that wouldn't last. He could see headlights coming around the corner a few blocks back.

"Jimmy!" she gasped in mock outrage.

He plunged a finger into her. She was so wet! Then he pulled it back to stroke her clit roughly before pushing it deep inside her again. He felt her shudder. Not a climax, but she was getting close. And so was he, damn it!

"We're not even going to make it into the house, Nicky. As soon as—"

"Drive fast!" she gasped as she pushed him back toward the wheel. "But I'm not waiting." And then she returned to stroking herself.

His one touch of her had been a mistake. It was hard enough listening to her excite herself. Those short gasps were the worst/best, as if she surprised herself with how aroused she was. Every time she made that little sound he nearly creamed himself. But he'd touched her, too, and her moisture was still coating his finger. He kept stroking his fingers together as if it were her. It was all he could do given that he was speeding down suburban streets in the middle of the night.

"This is not safe!" he ground out, hoping to slow her down.

"Do you want to be in me right now? Do you want to be screaming my name when the rush hits?"

"Yes! God, Nicky, you're killing me!"

"Ah…ah…oh, Jimmy!"

She screamed his name. She screamed his name and came while he was rounding the corner to his driveway. He'd never heard anything so damn sexy in his life. He jammed his thumb onto the button of the garage door opener, then he watched her while the thing climbed slowly open.

She was still undulating, though the motions were smaller and smaller. Her dress was off her shoulders, her breasts lifted high in the darkness. Her head was back, her neck exposed, and her mouth was parted in obvious bliss. Her hands were now resting, one on her belly, the other just above her knee. She looked like a woman who had just been well pleasured, and the sight was incredibly erotic. Not just because she was beautiful and obviously suffused with bliss, but because she'd come calling his name. His name.

"You can call me Jimmy anytime," he said.

She smiled and didn't even open her eyes. "Okay, Jimmy, how fast can you get a condom on?"

He slammed the car into the garage, hit the down button and was out of the Corvette before the garage door had done more than grind to life. He had a condom out of his wallet by the time he'd made it to her side of the car. In one smooth motion, he opened her door and jerked her out. Thank god she'd unfastened her seat belt. He was challenged enough managing the buttons on his tux.

She laughed seeing his condition, but she didn't offer to help. Instead, she stepped away from the car, turned her back on him, and slowly unzipped her dress from the top to the bottom in one long rrrrrrrrrr. The sound went straight down his spine and into his dick. He had no blood left anywhere else in his body. Meanwhile, she stepped out of her dress and ran a hand along the hood of his car.

"I've always wanted to be the girl on top of a Corvette. You know, the one in the pictures with her breasts hanging out and her bottom thrust up."

His pants were off. Hallelujah! He would have taken her then, but she'd said he always kept her safe. Safe meant condom. Condom meant more hand coordination. Bloody hell! Who designed these fracking foil packages?

Meanwhile, she'd boosted herself up onto his hood. She slid around to the front before he could manage the latex, then planted her stilettos on either side of his bumper, just inside the headlights, and slowly, coyly, rolled her spine down onto the hood of his car. She even lifted her hair so that it spilled gorgeously over his windshield.

Stilettos. Thigh-highs. Naked Nicky. On the hood of his car. Then she turned and looked at him.

"Do I look like a pinup?"

He used the last of his coordination to strip off his clothes. "You're going to come on the hood of my car," he rasped. "And then you're going to do it again and again until you scream my name."

"Pinups don't scream. They're silent."

He shook his head. "Not you. I'm the hypnotist, remember? You're going to scream."

"You're my island god," she said as she watched him come close.

He stalked to the front of his car, grabbed hold of her legs and jerked her forward. He entered her at the same time. It was an incredible feat of dexterity or luck; he wasn't sure which. He didn't care. It was so sudden she gave one of those squeaking gasps again and he lost it completely.

He drove into her like a machine, hard and fast and without regard for her. He might have felt guilty but she didn't seem to mind. She wrapped her legs around his ass and squeezed tight. The first spasms took him when her legs gripped him like a vise. He came like a geyser, but he didn't stop. He *couldn't* stop.

He felt the wave hit her with his next thrust. She convulsed around him and everything but her head rose off the hood. But she didn't scream his name. He had no thoughts beyond the wrack of pleasure and that one fact—she hadn't screamed his name and he wanted to hear it. His name in ecstasy.

"My name," he gasped. "Say my name."

Her breath was coming in time to his thrusts, but no words emerged.

"My name! I order it!" He used the same commanding tone he'd used two nights ago. His words were infused with every fiber of his being, and she responded as if she was still under hypnosis.

"Jimmy!" she cried as her body convulsed. "Jimmy!"

Her spasms pulled what was left in him out. Every drop went to her. Every part of his soul felt as if it went as well, poured into the amazing Nicky. He might have whispered those very words as he collapsed beside her.

He didn't know how long he lay there. Minutes. Hours. Didn't matter. There wasn't any part of him that didn't need aeons of recovery. But eventually he felt her shift and he opened his eyes. She lay sprawled across the hood of his car, and he had never seen anything more beautiful.

"It's hard work providing the perfect orgasms," he drawled. "I'm wiped out."

She arched a brow at him, but didn't say anything. Eventually a brain cell fired and he straightened up off his car. "Not the perfect orgasm?"

She shrugged. "It was very nice."

He studied her face and body. Her eyes were calm, her breathing relaxed. She had that air of absolute trust that only came when she was hypnotized, which meant he was more likely to get honest, open answers out of her.

"But it wasn't the perfect orgasm for you, was it?"

"No."

"What about before? Last night. On the…" What had she called it? "On your magical island? With all the men worshiping you as a goddess?"

Her lips curved into a sweet smile. "That was verrrry nice."

"But not perfect, huh?" Her silence was answer enough. "What would make it perfect?"

She blinked, obviously thinking. But in the end, she shrugged. "I don't know."

Right. As island god, it was his job to figure it out. Well, it was a tough assignment to be sure, but he wasn't about to quit. "Guess I'll just have to work harder at it, huh?"

She didn't answer, but he saw excitement spark in her eyes. And he wondered, abruptly, if she was still hypnotized. She certainly seemed alert and completely mentally aware. He was so caught up in his thoughts that he almost missed her next words.

"Maybe I can help some," she said. Then she gestured about his elaborate garage/workroom. "This is quite the setup."

He flushed. "Um. Yeah. Tinkering takes a lot of equipment." Then, unable to stop himself, he reached out and stroked her cheek. She closed her eyes to better appreciate the sensation, which gave him more moments to revel in the softness of her skin, the warmth of her body and the fact that she was right here with him.

What would he give to have her like this all the time? To come home every night to her in his home, in his bed, on his car. What was it worth to him?

Everything.

"Want to see more?" he asked, even though that was night and day from what he meant to say.

She grinned. "Oh yeah."

16

NICKY LOOKED ABOUT HER, feeling relaxed and intrigued by all of Jim's toys. He was right. Tinkering did take a lot of equipment. She couldn't keep track of all the gizmos that did stuff. Electronics, computers, gears and wires. She'd thought he'd made his millions on his brilliant idea, then kept himself occupied by consulting. That was certainly true, but in the downtime, Jim was either working on his next great idea or building illusions, some for himself, some for the people he called "real magicians." Which meant that his garage housed his Corvette on one side and a whole magic playhouse on the other side.

She had been on his "water" table Friday night. He generally used it for water illusions, but had a different top and hood set up for fire effects. Hoses dangled from pipes—hot and cold taps—which had given her the sensations she'd so enjoyed. He also had a disappearing-assistant coffin, a large cage, plus drapes, chains and a large array of fake weapons.

"This just rocks!" she said.

He nodded, his eyes steady and his expression careful. Throughout the tour, he kept looking at her oddly, frowning as he studied her. She guessed he was wondering if she were still hypnotized or fully conscious. Good question. She wasn't entirely sure herself. After all, she felt relaxed and happy as she hadn't in so long. It was as if tonight's date had brought back a slice of herself that she'd lost long ago.

Sure, the sex was part of it. Maybe a big part given how long it had been since she'd had a release, so to speak, but that wasn't what she'd rediscovered tonight. Jimmy made her remember who she'd been. He'd reminded her of the confidence she'd once had, her joyous belief that the future held good things. How had she lost that? Sure, life wasn't all kudos and roses, but it wasn't endless hours of work with no reward either. Or it shouldn't be. Being with Jim tonight had shown her so clearly how much she'd lost in the daily grind of her life.

And also that she'd clearly turned into a sex freak. Ideas were bursting in her brain. He certainly didn't describe anything in kinky terms, but her mind easily turned everything into Nicky's sexual playhouse. She saw potential toys in the most mundane things. And wow, did she want to try them all.

"I've become quite the sex kitten, haven't I?" she murmured to herself.

She hadn't meant for him to hear her, but he obviously did. So he leaned back against one of his worktables and folded his arms.

"That surprise you?" he asked.

"Totally," she answered with complete honesty. "It's been so long, I figured I'd regrown my virginity."

"You don't do things by halves, do you?"

"Apparently not." She mimicked his pose, a casual

lean against a table with her arms folded beneath her breasts. He'd pulled on his pants, but was still bare chested. A look she very much appreciated. She'd zipped back on her dress, but hadn't hooked anything. It would be the work of a moment to strip it right back off.

She could see he was thinking the same things she was. His eyes were alive with interest and her body was already wet and willing. But it was well past midnight. Even if Mr. Millionaire Consultant didn't have to get up early tomorrow, she certainly did. Reports to compile, factory shipments to juggle, a thousand jobs to *not* lay off.

"I need to get back home," she said reluctantly.

"Yeah, I figured." He moved to where his shirt dangled from bicycle handlebars. No bike, just the handlebars propped on a table. "But I'd really like to see you again. Think we could manage a second date?"

He kept his voice casual, and she found herself responding to his light tone. "I think I could manage that." A second, a third, and probably up to a fifty-ninth date, given all the possibilities she saw in his workshop. And that didn't even include the things that could be done in his house.

"Gawd," she drawled as she watched him pull on his shirt, "I want to be a millionaire so that I can hang out all day and play."

"What would you do?"

"Besides have sex with you until my head explodes? Work out. Get a tan. I don't know. Do stuff."

He nodded, absently buttoning his shirt. He didn't need to speak for her to know what he was thinking.

"You think I'd get bored. You think I can't even take a vacation without going nuts."

He arched a brow back at her. "Can you?"

"Of course I can!" she said. But then she thought back to her last few vacations. Sure they'd started out great. But two days into a weeklong break and…well, she'd started getting twitchy. "Okay, so I like working," she finally confessed. "So do you, apparently. You could be relaxing on your millions, but here you are, contracting out to the guy who bought your design, working up your next brilliant discovery, and tooling illusions in your spare time. Hardly—umph!"

He picked her up—physically lifted her right off the floor—then spun her around until she landed, *plop,* right down on a table draped in black velvet.

"You seem to think I want you to change. We've barely had our first date, and yet I'm supposedly thinking all this stuff about how you need to be different." He planted a hot kiss on her lips. "Really, Nicky, I think you're great just as you are."

She was flushed and hot, an all too common state for her these days, and was completely speechless. Fortunately, he didn't give her a chance to stutter something awkward, something that made no sense. He caressed her cheek and then pinched her chin when her eyes started drifting closed.

"I'm not judging you, Nicky. I never have."

She let her head drop forward onto his. He met it and held, his breath a hot caress against her lips. It was a strangely intimate position. There was no posturing in the moment. She wasn't trying to be a badass boss or a brain-dead submissive. It was just her without pretense touching him without expectations. And in this place, she finally voiced the truth.

"*I* think I need to change. I just don't know how to do it yet."

He nodded, and because they were forehead to

forehead, her head moved as well. "I'd like to help you work it out," he said softly.

"Well, endless orgasms do seem to be helping," she drawled.

He heaved an overly dramatic sigh. "Well, if that's what it takes, I suppose I can offer myself up as stud…"

She chuckled at his dry tone, but then slowly sobered. She wanted so much more from him than stud services. But how much? And would she end up being disappointed? And…

"Your body's tightening up again."

"Want to hypnotize me again?"

He pulled back, his eyes serious. "I want to know what happened, Nicky. Why are you running so scared all the time?"

She huffed. "You seem to think it was one event. It wasn't. I got to college and it was hard, so I worked harder. I got into the job market, and it was really hard. I connected up with two…no three different guys, each time thinking they were the man for me. They weren't—"

"Why?"

She huffed. "Same reason the wrestler in high school was such a bad prom date choice. He had credentials, Jimmy. He was captain of the wrestling team, looked hot in those little shorts, and was a big man in high school."

"I remember."

"But in private, he was an ass. At prom, he was a drunken ass."

"Which is why I found you walking home alone with a ripped dress."

She smiled at the memory. "He didn't hurt me. None

of them did. They were just bad choices." And the last one had been the absolute worst.

"And they shook your confidence."

Understatement of the year. "Then I borrowed money to go to graduate school."

"But you did it. You got your degree."

She nodded, but he didn't know how hard she'd worked for just mediocre grades. She wasn't the top of her class, she was barely in the middle. "There was so much debt, Jimmy. I borrowed from the bank, from my parents, from Susan and her husband, too." Then the asshole boyfriend had wiped out her accounts. "I just…I had to get a good job."

"You got one."

She nodded. She got one, she'd paid everyone off, but she'd never loved what she did. She was only paying back debts. And once they were paid off, she wanted to get a good cushion in her bank account so she'd never have to face that kind of financial terror again. "I'm so afraid I'm going to end up back on the street."

He stiffened. "Back?"

She nodded. "I was homeless for a couple weeks. Not long. I was the only one in the shelter going to graduate school." She tried for a laugh, but it didn't sound very convincing. "My last bad choice got access to my bank account. He cleaned me out, then skipped."

"Oh my god, Nicky." His hands stroked her arms, his fingers clenching reflexively.

"I had already borrowed so much from my family, I couldn't go back to them. Plus, I was embarrassed. They still don't know. Anyway, he'd been pocketing the rent money. By the time I found out, I was months behind."

"Evicted?"

"Oh yeah. Stuff on the curb and all. I sold everything I owned to finish school and eventually imposed on an old friend from college to sleep on her couch. But for a while there I didn't have a place to live."

"So you went to a shelter? Nicky—"

"Don't pity me, Jimmy!" she said sharply. "I worked my way out of it. I've paid back every cent. I've earned—"

He silenced her with a swift, deep kiss. And when he was done, he pulled back to look deep into her eyes. "I don't pity you, Nicky. I'm impressed as hell. I knew you were strong, but damn, most people would have broken under that kind of pressure. You've come out tougher, better, more capable than ever."

She release a soft laugh, feeling years of stress slide away. He understood. "I'm doing okay now," she said. "My bank account is solid, my résumé is good."

"But you're still afraid," he said. It wasn't a question. He knew she was.

She lifted her chin. "Except with you. Except when—"

"You're hypnotized."

She laughed. "I was going to say multi-orgasmic, but okay. We'll go with hypnotized."

He touched her cheek. "You can't spend your entire life under hypnosis, Nicky. When are you going to let go of the fear and let yourself live?"

She didn't answer because she didn't know. All she could think was that she wasn't afraid when she was with him. When he looked at her as he was now, she remembered the girl she'd been. She remembered to believe in herself and that life could be good. But she couldn't manage to say that aloud just then. It was too revealing, and she'd just told him so very much more than anyone else knew. So she just looked at him, and he at her.

And after a minute like this, the moment became too intense. The sexual tension was nothing compared to the quiet need to be in his arms, to be held and nurtured and just touched gently. The yearning built and built inside her head until she had to jerk backward or rush headlong into his arms forever.

"I gotta go," she said, rushing her words. "Work. Reports. Career. You know—"

"I know," he said, and there was acceptance in his expression. "I know," he repeated softly. And for a frozen moment, she realized he truly did know. He understood her fears and her need for space. He realized that she needed to become comfortable with their new intimacy before she allowed them anything more between them. So he shuttered his expression and gestured to his car.

"I…uh…I'll drive you home."

"Uh, yeah," she said as she leaped off the velvet. "Thanks." She got into his car as he hit the garage door button. Then he climbed into the driver's side, accidentally revving the car before backing out.

They drove in silence, making it to her condo in what had to be record time. She turned her face to stare at the patterns of light and shadow that made up the Chicago skyline. Had she just ruined a perfect night with her own insecurities? Had her confessions turned him sour on her? She didn't think so, but she couldn't shake the nagging fear that dogged her every thought. If it wasn't the terror of being homeless, it was the fear that she'd made yet another disastrous choice in men. Sure, he felt like the best thing to happen to her in ages, but was he really? Was he going to empty her bank accounts, too?

She knew her fears were ridiculous, but she couldn't make them go away. And she couldn't bring back the hypnosis either. Truthfully, the line between consciousness and hypnotized was getting more blurry every time she saw him. Was she hypnotized when he smiled at her and made her fears go away? Or was she simply reacting to him? To how wonderful he made her feel? She closed her eyes and felt stupid. This was case and point why she never dated.

"I had a great time tonight, Nicky. Even before the... you know, Corvette thing."

She smiled as his voice filled the dark interior. He was soft spoken, his low tones slipping beneath her skin almost on the same level as the growl of the engine. It was his hypnotist voice—or maybe it was just his quiet voice. Either way, she felt her fears ease as she rolled her head back to look at him.

"I like you a lot, Jimmy. Er, Jim."

He grinned. "I've become fond of the name Jimmy again. Feel free to use it. You can even scream it."

She smiled back, remembering exactly when and how she had screamed that name. She wasn't sure how she could handle intimacy with him, a real relationship with give and take and intimate confessions. But sex? Fantasy playland? She could handle that. She *wanted* that. "So, was I good enough that I get a second date?"

"I can take you out to someplace fancy. We've done the nostalgia thing. How about downtown? Something classy?"

"How about pizza and your magic room?"

He arched a brow. "Magic room?"

"You prefer I call it your sexual playhouse?"

He choked. "No, magic room works great. Whatever you want, Nicky. I—"

"Tomorrow night. I'll be done at work by six. Er…six-thirty." She huffed. "Hell. Better make that seven."

"Seven," he said as he caught her hand and brought it to his lips. "But not a minute later."

The kiss goodbye wasn't hot, or rather it didn't start out that way. He simply touched her mouth, stroked it a bit with his tongue while his fingers burrowed into her hair. Not demanding. Not a prelude to hot and heavy. But it was nice, and it continued to be nice. And then nicer.

When was the last time she'd made out in the front seat of a car? Never! And yet…it was good. It was great!

"This is nuts," she whispered to the fogged windows. She didn't even have the strength to roll her head to look at him.

"Yeah, but if this is a loony bin, I don't feel like leaving."

"Me, neither," she returned. "Tomorrow morning is going to suck."

"Yeah," he agreed. "I'm conference calling with NY at eight a.m."

"I have to figure out which four hundred employees to lay off."

He jerked. She felt it even though she wasn't looking at him. "Seriously? Four hundred?"

She bit her lip. "I wasn't, um, supposed to say that. Because our company isn't in bad financial straits at all," she lied.

"Of course not," he said, obviously understanding the message underneath.

"But, hypothetically, if we did have to lay off people, it would be my job to figure out how to make it the least painful. It started out as close to a thousand. I've worked the numbers down to about four hundred. That's what I was doing all weekend."

"I didn't realize…" He shook his head. "No wonder you've been about to explode."

Even in the darkness, she could see that his brow was furrowed with thought. "Yeah, that's me. Corporate hatchet woman."

He shook his head. "I didn't realize how high up in the corporate structure you are. You said middle management."

"I am—"

"Not if you're making layoff reports."

She liked that he understood the responsibilities she had. Her title in no way reflected what she did every day. "Put it this way. My boss makes the actual decision. But he does it off the reports I give him."

"That puts a lot of pressure on you."

She lifted her head off the leather seat. He was saying something here. He was having a lightbulb moment, but she hadn't a clue what he'd figured out. "What?" she pressed.

"Nothing," he hedged, but at her look, he continued. "I just wonder if this sex fest is you blowing off steam, that's all. Are you going to disappear once the job pressure eases?"

She laughed. "No worries there. My job pressure never eases." And with that, she pressed a quick kiss to his lips. She wanted to deepen it. She wanted to have him drive her right back to his place where they would play for another twenty years. But she forced herself away.

"G'night," she said. Then she blew him a kiss and shut the car door. But her mind wouldn't leave him. By the time she made it up to her condo, she had the beginnings of three different fantasy scenarios. By the time she got into bed, she was humming with anticipation.

Tomorrow day was going to suck. Tomorrow night, on the other hand, was going to make it all worthwhile.

JIM COULDN'T STOP THINKING. His mind churned all through the drive home and then well into the night. He shouldn't have bothered going to bed at all. He tossed and turned until his bed was a twisted mass of sheets and tortured thoughts.

He was just sex relief for her. Their whole relationship was based on hypnotized hot and horny. Great, but after an evening spent talking to her, he already knew he wanted more.

She was bright, funny, hardworking and drop-dead gorgeous. Jeez, she'd been homeless, but had worked herself right out of debt. She obviously thought she wasn't very smart. That she had to work herself to death because she wasn't brilliant enough to see the better way out. But he knew that hard work trumped brains any day. Take him, for example—his great idea was only one tiny fraction of what it had taken to build his company. Success came in working out the details, and that required sweat and discipline. And that, obviously, she possessed in spades.

She was everything he wanted in a woman. Everything he wanted in the mother of his children, too— and that thought had him sitting bolt upright in a cold sweat.

They'd reconnected only a few days ago. He couldn't possibly be thinking the whole package with her. Except, he was. Marriage, children, the whole shebang. With

Nicky. A woman who had to be hypnotized into having sex with him.

Oh my God, he was depraved. He wanted to marry a woman who was into bondage and who knew what else. He wanted to father children with a woman who thought of him as a super-duper sex toy. One who came with a Corvette and a magic sex room.

What was wrong with him? And yet, how could he stop?

Okay, he thought as he finally pushed out of bed. Time for a logic tree or at least a pro/con list. Pro: Nicky was the full package. He wanted her the way he wanted his next breath. Con: She only viewed him as a sex toy. Pro: She was into exploring every sexual fantasy he had. And many he hadn't even thought of. Con: He was just her sex toy. And she had to be hypnotized into that. Pro: He was getting laid multiple times a night. Con: He very much feared that was all he was going to get from her.

In short, they related great on the sexual level. But if he wanted a relationship with her—and he did—then they needed to move out of his magic room and into a different arena. Family. Friends. A relationship. But how?

It took him another ten minutes, but he finally had an idea. He turned on his laptop and shot off a quick e-mail to his brother.

17

"YOU INVITED YOUR MOTHER to dinner?" Nicky asked as they walked toward a large table. Nicky was wearing a black leather bustier and matching thong beneath blousy piratelike pants. She was hoping for a *Pirates of the Caribbean* fantasy, though she'd also been thinking about dog collars and whips. Not sure yet if she wanted to go there, but she'd spent her entire seventeen minutes of lunch surfing through Web sites that made her blush. She'd managed to swing by the Leather and Stud shop on the way home to buy her current attire. Fortunately, she had a blouse and jacket on to cover the sex-kitten corset, but she was excruciatingly aware of it.

And now she was walking through a quaint Italian restaurant to a dinner with his mother? The mental whiplash was too much too process. And it got worse the minute she saw the other dinner guests.

"You invited *my* family, too?" she gasped. She'd been thinking kinky, and he'd given her Sunday after church.

"I didn't mean to," he said, an apology in every word. "I swear I didn't. I just talked to my brother, Rick, this morning and mentioned pizza. He said great, and then before I knew it my mother called to say she'd join us. I tried to call you, but it kept going to voice mail—"

"I had to turn it off." Nicky's hands started clenching, putting creases in her black pants. Good lord, she was wearing a thong! "My mother is here!" she said with a hiss. "You didn't call my mother, did you?"

"God, no! But, um, weird thing that. Rick, um, knows your sister Tammy. And she—"

"Tammy's coming? Do you see what I'm wearing?" Hysteria was creeping into her voice.

"I know. I know, but…I mean, I *didn't* know this would happen. Rick called Tammy who called—"

"Everybody! That's what Tammy does. She calls *everybody!*" Nicky was already turning around. There was still time to duck away. Nobody had seen her yet. At a minimum, she could rush home and change before—

"There you are, Nicky! You didn't tell me you were dating anyone!" It was her sister Susan, complete with husband Brian and baby Emily. "Come give your godchild a kiss before she spits up and ruins the mood."

Nicky turned back to the group, her cheeks heating to inferno level. She managed to shoot Jim a glare, but then pasted on a tight smile. "Hi, Susan. I didn't realize you were coming."

"Yeah, well, you would have if you'd read my e-mail—"

"I was working!" she ground out. She hadn't had time to look at her e-mail. She'd spent her entire day either in meetings or running numbers. Then there was the quick stop by the shop with barely enough time to change before driving here. She bent over to kiss Emily's forehead, inhaling the sweet scent of baby and talcum.

She didn't dare take the child. She'd squeeze the poor kid to death. "Hey, sweetie," she murmured.

"Quite the new look," her sister drawled while Nicky was still bent over.

Nicky straightened so fast she nearly lost her footing. "I didn't realize anyone else was coming!"

"Uh, Nicky," interrupted Jim with an awkward cough. "I'd, uh, like to introduce you to my mother."

"Hello, Mrs. Ray. Pleased to meet you." Nicky smiled and wished she could sink into the floor. That or whip one of the checked tablecloths off the table and wrap it around herself like a toga.

"I hope you don't mind me horning in like this, but I get out so little that I tend to seize the opportunity when I can. And it's been so long since I saw your family."

"Over ten years," Nicky said as she forced a smile. "We've got quite the group here. Hello, Mom. Do you like to garden, Mrs. Ray? My mom is always doing stuff with her plants. What was that rare flower you're cultivating—"

"That was last year, dear," her mother said as she dropped a kiss on her cheek. "This year's experiment is with bushes. I'm trying to see if I can hide that ugly air conditioner with—"

"Squee! Look at my sister out of a business suit! Wow, do you look hot!"

Nicky turned around to give a pained look at her sister Tammy. "Did you have to invite *everyone?*" she bit out as they hugged.

"To meet your new boyfriend? Hell, yes. This is the event of the century!" Tammy shot back, completely unrepentant.

Fortunately for Tammy, Nicky didn't have the chance to strangle her. Rick showed up, and then the baby started crying. Food had to be ordered next, and then the wine came. Thank God for the wine. And on it continued through salad and pizza.

Jim's mom did indeed like to garden, though she wasn't as avid about it as Nicky's mom. Rick and Tammy had some strange chemistry going. They were apparently old friends, but most of their bickering centered on a girl named Corine. And Susan was obviously happy as an exhausted mom. Nicky was halfway to jealous of her sister's baby, loving husband and the whole happily-ever-after thing until Jim chose that moment to help her off with her jacket. Not a big deal, but he was close enough to see the bustier beneath the demure peach silk blouse.

His eyes shot wide, and his face heated to blistering. Hers, too, for that matter.

"I'm so sorry," he murmured as he eased her jacket off her arms.

"It's fine," she finally said, though it took a moment for her to get the words out. "These things happen. Usually to Tammy, but I suppose it was my turn."

"Nicky—" he began, but she cut him off. There would be plenty of time for explanations later. Right then, they had to get through this meal.

"So, Mom," she said, turning away from Jim. "Is Dad enjoying his trip?"

"Oh, you know these academic conferences. Always in someplace fun, but I couldn't go because…"

"I'M SO SORRY," Jim repeated for the thousandth time as he opened the Corvette's door for her. "I just thought it'd be fun for you to meet Rick. He's laid back and really cool. I just didn't think—"

"It wasn't time for relatives," she said as she settled into the leather seats of his car. She'd taken a cab to the restaurant, since she hadn't wanted to be separated from him even in the short drive to his home.

"I know—"

"It wasn't even time for your brother. No relatives. Not yet." Nicky wasn't exactly sure why she was holding on to her anger so fiercely. In truth, he hadn't done anything but have a family meal get out of hand. And when *hadn't* that happened with her family? But she was angry and panicking. Why?

Rather than answer that, she turned abruptly toward him. He'd barely sat down in the car when she grabbed his arm and spoke in a rush. "Hypnotize me. Right now."

He frowned, his eyes narrowing rather than widening as they did when he wanted to put her under. She tightened her grip, but he shook his head. "Nicky, we have to talk," he began, but it was interrupted by his brother's rap on the trunk. He whipped around to glare at Rick, but then had to roll down the window when his brother didn't move from the car door.

"What?"

"Sorry, bro. Didn't mean to make it such a nut-fest."

"Yeah, I know."

Rick looked directly at Nicky. "Don't blame him. It was all my fault."

She nodded, but her eyes were on Jim. His hands were clenched on the steering wheel and his shoulders were tensed up to his ears. She sighed and turned to Rick. "Don't worry about it. I think the problem runs deeper than family nut-fest."

Rick arched a dark eyebrow. He looked as if he

wanted to say something, but in the end he just shrugged. "I guess I'll be moving on, then. Night."

"Night," she and Jim answered together.

They stared out at the parking lot as one after another of their family members pulled away. Susan and family went first in their minivan. Tammy had her little Prius, then the moms departed in classic sedans. Finally Rick peeled out in a Mazda, which left her and Jim still sitting in the parking lot.

"They're gone," she said when he still didn't turn to her. "You can do it now."

"Hypnotize you?" he asked, still not looking at her.

She caught the tight note in his voice and his hands still hadn't unclenched on the wheel. The tightness in her chest racheted up another notch. "Or you could tell me what's really going on. Please."

"I want more," he said, rushing his words. Then he turned to look directly at her. "I know it's fast. It's freaking me out how fast. But I want more of you than just hypnotized sex."

"So you invited the whole clan along on a date? Because...why?" She already knew the answer. It was obvious now that he was looking for family—a wife, children, probably the whole shebang. But the very idea was preposterous. She could barely fit in time for a date, much less...more.

He sighed. "I didn't mean it to be that many people."

"I had a whole schedule worked out," she said softly. Then for proof, she pulled a list out of her purse. It was the fantasies she wanted to try. One for each night except for Thursday. She had a big meeting on Friday and figured she'd really need her sleep by then.

He looked at the page, his eyes shooting wide. And

then he choked. "You really wanted to try this on Saturday?"

"Only as part of this scenario I got off the Internet. I just thought...you know, why not see if we like it?"

"So tonight's *Pirates of the Caribbean* was just a warm-up to next week?"

She flushed scarlet, reaching out to pull the page out of his hand. He didn't give it up. In fact, he folded it away into his jeans pocket, and she wasn't going to fight to get it back. Not right now. Though she could tell by the thickening bulge in his pants that he was interested. It didn't matter. By introducing his family, everything had gotten really complicated, really fast.

She turned away. "I'm not ready for anything else. I've got a career, and babies spit up on designer suits. They pee on things, too, and don't sleep through the night." She said the words, but inside, her heart ached. She did want babies sometime. And the thought of Jim's babies wasn't so very bad. In fact, it was kind of a lovely thought. They'd probably be wickedly smart. She'd teach them not to be so shy, and if they had a laugh like his— all sexy, deep and throaty—then there was nothing those kids couldn't do.

"I didn't say anything about babies, Nicky." His voice was soft, but it seemed to throb in her head. "I just wanted to know if we could relate on a different level. On one that didn't include—"

"Pirates? Leather thongs?"

His eyebrows shot up into his hairline. "You're wearing a leather thong?"

"Yes. While I was sitting across from your mother talking tulips."

He swallowed. She heard it distinctly. "That is so hot. That...that is so hot it's short-circuiting my brain."

She shook her head. "No, it's not hot. It's...sick. I'm not mixing leather and your mother. Not ever."

"Oh, yuck. Oh god, no."

"Exactly." She took a deep breath and turned her face away from him to stare out at another massive family group disgorging from the restaurant. Papa Georgio's Pizzeria apparently did quite the business in family get-togethers.

"I think I need to go home, Jim."

"Nicky..." he began, but he didn't finish. He just looked at her in mute appeal.

"I can't reconcile the two. What we do together—what we did—and..." She gestured weakly to a family of five climbing out of another minivan. Mom, Dad and three chattering school-aged kids. "They don't go together in my brain. You have to hypnotize it out. It's the only way."

"Why?"

She looked at him, saw the challenge in his eyes, and immediately lost the ability to breathe. Her chest constricted that far.

"You're afraid," he said. "I get that. But you know you're—"

He almost said the words. She felt them, hovering in the air. He was about to say that she was safe with him, but he stopped before uttering her trigger words. If only he just said the words, then she would go under. She knew it. But he didn't, and the lack of that reassurance cut deep. It wasn't rational, but she couldn't stop the question. Was she safe with him?

She sighed and turned to stare out the window. "Take me home, please. I'm tired and I have a lot—"

"Of work to do," he finished for her. "Yeah. What a shock."

18

"TEN BUCKS SAYS you just screwed up the best thing that's ever happened to you."

Jim looked up from his garage worktable. It was midafternoon on a glorious spring day. The garage door was up, letting in sunlight, birdsong and his brother, Rick.

"What?" he said, though he'd heard every word.

"I said, you screwed the pooch on this one. Fracked the goat. Been a big—"

"I got it. I got it." He pushed back from his table and glared at his brother's silhouette as Rick moved through the maze to the worktable. "And you're wrong. This was not my fault. She and I...well, we just didn't fit." It was a lie, of course. But it was a lie he'd been telling himself all morning, and so he was rather attached to it at the moment.

"Uh-huh. So tell me more." Rick leaned back against the edge of the water table. The very table where Nicky had...

"You're not a shrink, Rick. You own a nightclub and

sometimes tend bar. That does not give you a free pass into my brain."

"Don't need a pass. I'm your brother."

Jim didn't say anything. He just shrugged and looked away. But Rick had a way about him, a silent presence that made even the most closemouthed patron slowly sputter into speech. And for all his posturing, Jim was no different. After a minute or two of silence, he spun back to his desk and started talking. He picked up a pen and started doodling, too, but it was his mouth that was really running.

"I've been lonely lately, you know," he said. "I work alone, I live alone. I even consult in e-mail now. Don't even talk to people over the phone. The most contact I get in the human world is amateur night, and that's not people. That's performing."

"The answer to loneliness is to get out and meet people."

He nodded. "I know. And I was starting. And then, wham, Nicky's right there sitting on my front porch."

"Yeah, uh, remind me how that happened. Last thing I knew you were getting drunk and moaning about how the high school volleyball player didn't even remember you. And then bam, she's your pizza-night date and looking hotter than the latest issue of *Corporate Babe*."

Jim arched a brow. "You do not seriously read that magazine, do you?"

Rick shrugged. "It's not a magazine that is usually *read*."

There was no answer to that. "I'm tired of living through the Internet and in this garage. I'm ready for something more." He looked up at his brother. "I want a wife, kids, the whole nuclear family."

"And you thought Nicky was a piece of that package."

He shrugged. "Yeah, maybe. I mean, we fit in certain ways." He prayed he wasn't blushing too red. "But I didn't know if we could do the rest. The family thing."

"And what did she say? Does she want a family? From what Tammy says, she's corporate track the whole way."

Jim didn't answer. He'd filled up his piece of paper anyway, so he busied himself with ripping off the sheet of doodles and throwing it away. Rick, of course, wasn't in the least bit fooled.

"You didn't even talk to her about this, did you? You just created pizza night and were surprised when it blew up in your face." Rick laughed. "God, for a genius, you sure are a moron."

"I just wanted to know—"

"If she fit. Yeah, I heard." Rick leaned down and grabbed the crumpled piece of notepaper out of the garbage. He smoothed it out and inspected the lines and squiggles. "You know, Jimmy, you can see patterns where other people just see scribbles."

"Actually, those *are* just scribbles—"

"Listen to me, moron. I'm about to give you a life lesson."

"You do know that you're the younger brother, right? I'm supposed to educate you."

"Yeah, well, when I decide to go back to school, you can be the instructor. Right now, I'm the one with all the experience."

Jim thought about arguing, but his younger brother *was* ten times more experienced with women than he was. "Fine, Obi-Wan. What does the Force have to say on my love life?"

"That you have this pattern in your head of what you want, and you're looking for the right pieces to drop into it. Buddy, that's not love, that's a jigsaw puzzle. If you want a wife and family, you better start with talking to the woman and finding out what she wants."

"Sex. More sex. And only sex." And she had to be hypnotized into that. He pulled out Nicky's fantasy schedule and handed it over. Then he immediately regretted the action. This was more than he wanted to share with anyone, but it was too late. His brother had already scanned the list and let out a low whistle.

"Um, wow. I think I need a cold shower."

"She is the hottest woman in bed I've ever had. That I've ever imagined." He pulled the schedule back and tucked it carefully back in his pocket.

"Jeez, man, if you don't want her, can I have her?"

"Touch her, talk to her, and I swear to God, Rick, I will gut you from nose to dick."

It took a moment of stunned silence for Jim to realize what he'd just said. Even longer for him to absorb his absolute raw fury at the idea of his brother—of anyone—getting near Nicky. Of doing anything on her list with her.

"Jesus, I'm a Neanderthal," he moaned.

He looked up to see his brother smile. Rick didn't do that often, not the full-blown grin that transformed his flat face into something verging on handsome. But he was grinning right now, and Jim just rolled his eyes. "Did you come here for a reason? Or just to torture me?"

"Just wanted to know how deep you'd fallen, big brother."

"What are you talking about?"

"In love, moron. You're in love with Nicky." Then he gestured at the pocket that held Nicky's sex schedule. "Hell, after seeing that, I think I'm in love, too."

"Get the hell out of here."

"Not yet. One last piece of advice. She's a person, Jimmy. You gotta see her as a person who has her own schedule and thoughts and patterns."

Jim arched a brow at his brother. "And tell me again how many happy, committed relationships you've had."

"Those who can't do…teach." He grabbed the phone from the far side of the desk and passed it to Jim. "Send her flowers, then call her. Tell her you were an ass and you want to start again. Grovel like a worm."

"I told you," Jim snapped, his temper getting the best of him. "She doesn't want more. And look, I like sex as much as the next guy, but…" He shook his head. "What if she doesn't want more ever?"

Rick laughed. "Every woman does eventually. You just have to show her you're the guy who can give it to her."

Jim slumped, the fight and the anger going out of him. "But how? I've been thinking about it all night. How do I convince her?"

Rick shrugged. "Groveling is all I got, buddy. Anything beyond that, and you're on your own."

NICKY LOOKED AT THE FLOWERS on her desk. Two dozen red roses. Just days old and they were starting to wilt. She reached up to stroke one dark red petal, taking a moment to revel in the softness against her skin. Then she leaned in to smell them and winced at the not-so-pleasant-anymore scent. Why didn't things last longer?

She picked up Jim's note. It was written in a girlish round scribble. She'd seen Jimmy's handwriting—a neat, block lettering reminiscent of an architect's—which meant this note had been written by the florist, but the message was all his.

"Date 3 will be better. Give me a chance. Please call me."

She'd e-mailed him instead. She'd told him she wasn't angry, she just had a lot of work to do and she'd contact him on the weekend. A cooling-off period was probably for the best anyway since things had been moving at light speed between them. She just needed to refocus on her career for the moment, and she'd get back to him soon.

That's what she'd said, and she'd meant it at the time. She really did have to figure things out. She'd managed to pare down the possible layoffs to a little over one hundred, but it was still crisis time at work. She had to stay focused.

It was all true, and it was also all a lie. It was *always* crisis time at work. Multimillion-dollar corporations always had something important going on that would affect thousands of people. Now was no different than any other day of the week. So why was she running scared? Why had she cut Jimmy off just because her pizza and fantasy play night had turned into family night?

She sighed. Even back in high school, Jimmy had known what he wanted and gone straight for it. He'd told her that night after prom that he was going to invent something special by the time he was twenty. That he would have his own company, and become a bajillion-aire by the time he was thirty.

She'd scoffed that night in the diner, but he'd gone out and done it. Everything he'd planned had come true for him. She, on the other hand, had managed exactly zero of her plans. She'd planned on a career in something environmental and meeting Mr. Right by the time she was twenty-five. She hadn't planned on getting cleaned out by her boyfriend, living in a homeless shelter or working her butt off in a plastics firm.

So what did that have to do with Jimmy? Only that he clearly wanted more than a nightly sex fest with her. It wasn't just family night. He was the one who'd wanted a first date and was now pleading for a third. Sure, she liked him. Sure, she wanted a relationship and a family…someday. But she didn't have the time just now, not for a full relationship.

She even wrote the words down on a piece of paper and placed it on top of his note so as to remind her of what was important.

"Career first. Get back to work."

So she did. Until her sister burst through her office door. Susan stomped in, planted her feet right in front of Nicky's desk and glared. She even planted her fists right on her hips. But she didn't say a word.

"Um…hello, Susan," Nicky said slowly. "What are you doing here so late on a Thursday night?"

"I don't know, Nicky. Why would I be here?"

None of the smart-ass remarks that came to mind would help matters, so Nicky kept her mouth shut.

"Okay, how's this?" snapped Susan. "You're fired as Emily's godmother."

Nicky's eyes widened. "Fired? But why?"

"Appointment with the priest? Tonight at five-thirty? Ring any bells?"

Nicky frowned, abruptly sifting through her piles

of papers to pull out her phone. "No. It was later in the week."

"Thursday *is* later in the week." Susan leaned forward. "*Today* is Thursday."

Nicky grabbed her phone and pulled up her schedule. "I put in three reminders so I wouldn't forget. I remember it specifically. I was driving to the bar and talking to you. You told me—"

"That you couldn't forget, Nicky. This was your last chance."

"I know! That's why I put in the reminders. Three of them..." She started punching buttons, paging through date after date of don't-forget messages and must-be-done-now notes. But in all that mass of notes, there wasn't one about the meeting with the priest. "Wait..."

Then she remembered. She'd been *driving*. She'd already had a few near-death experiences because she'd been typing in notes while driving. So she didn't put in the reminders then. She'd planned on doing it at the bar. She'd gone in intending to do it, but then Professor Thompson hadn't been there, so she had to e-mail him to try to reschedule. She'd planned on putting in the reminders right after that, but then Jimmy had swiped her phone. He was doing his Magic Man act. Then she'd been hypnotized, and...and...and she'd never gotten around to putting in the reminders.

"Oh god. I screwed up. Again."

"Yeah. You did."

She looked up at her sister, seeing the anger set in the tight lines of her mouth. Lord, the last time Susan had looked like that was when...when...crap. It was the last time Nicky had forgotten something important. Dad's birthday party. And before that, she'd missed the dress fittings for her wedding. Nicky had ended up at the ceremony in a bridesmaid's gown held together by pins.

"Susan, I am so, so sorry."

Her sister didn't respond. Instead, she leaned over and picked up Nicky's note, snorting as she read it. Then she turned it around and held it up for Nicky to see.

"Career first," she said. "Is there a number two? Family? Friends? A life? Is there any room on your list for anything like that?"

"Of course there is!" Nicky returned. "Just…well, just not now…" Her voice trailed away. In truth, her breath was shortening, her body tightening. Was she going to have a panic attack right now? Right here in front of her sister? She couldn't. She could *not!*

"Just not now." Susan echoed with a sigh, and it seemed as if the sound came from deep in her toes. Then she pulled up a chair—she had to set aside a pile of papers first—and plopped down across from her. "So, what about that guy Jimmy? From high school."

"He goes by Jim now."

"Okay. He sent you roses. He seemed like a nice guy. And Tammy says he's loaded. Some dot com millionaire."

"Engineering."

"Again…okay. So what's going on with you two?"

Nicky shifted awkwardly in her seat. "Nothing special," she lied.

Her sister wasn't fooled. "You on a date is special. You looking like a *Pirates of the Caribbean* sex slut is special."

"I did not look like a slut!" she gasped. "Please tell me I didn't look like—"

"You looked good. But I saw that leather corset. No

way is that part of your normal corporate uniform." She waved dismissively at Nicky's current attire: a dark blue suit with modest lapels and a tailored waist.

"Jimmy's good," she said slowly.

"I thought you said his name was Jim."

"It is. It's…it's complicated."

"Criminy, Nicky. Only you could make a man's name complicated!" She leaned over and picked up Jim's note. "So he's begging for date number three and you're suddenly buried in work. What a surprise…not."

Nicky felt her annoyance build. Sure, she was the one who had screwed up, but now Susan was mucking about in her rela…er, personal life. No way did she even want to think the word *relationship*.

"Look, I'm just so busy right now. I don't really have time…" She stopped when Susan held up her hand. Nicky might have argued, but when Susan got to lecturing, all she could do was wait it out.

"You weren't like this as a kid."

"Of course I was," she shot back, though she really had no idea what Susan was talking about.

"You were fun. You laughed and goofed off. But somewhere between high school and adulthood, all the fun got sucked out of you."

"I do have fun, you know."

"No, Nicky, you don't. You have benchmarks. This degree, this salary, this job, this amount in the bank. When did your life become a series of achievements?"

Nicky stared at her sister. It was as if Susan were talking an alien language. Yeah, she understood the words, but not the tone of disdain. "My degree, my job, my salary, they're all important," she said.

"More important than your goddaughter? More important than a boyfriend? What happened to you?"

Nicky just looked at her sister, feeling as if her mind and body were completely frozen. As if maybe, they had been frozen for a really long time and she hadn't even realized it. "Do you know what it's like to be homeless, Susan?"

Her sister snorted. "You're a long way from homeless, little sister."

Nicky just picked up her sign, turning it over and over in her hands. "Everything in you rebels. No, you can't be one of *those* people. You work hard. You aren't crazy. But there you are with nothing except debts, and it's getting dark. You actually think about sleeping on a park bench. You. A middle-class girl from a good family. And where do you go to the bathroom? Take a shower? What about when it gets cold? Suddenly these things are real and they're terrifying."

Susan expelled a long breath. Nicky didn't dare look at her. She didn't know what she feared. A look of pity? A sigh of acceptance, as if Nicky deserved the fate she'd had? Logically, she knew Susan would never do that to her. And yet, Nicky couldn't look. She could barely even breathe. Finally, her sister spoke. A single word, but it seemed to echo in the room.

"When?"

"Grad school and only for a little while."

"How?"

"Asshole boyfriend." She refused to even say the bastard's name out loud. "He'd been pocketing my rent money for a while. Then he cleaned out my bank account and skipped town. By the time I found out, I was being evicted."

"Why didn't you call me? We had money. Mom and Dad would have helped."

Nicky shook her head. "It happened so fast, Susan.

Yeah, there were signs, but I didn't see them. God, I was so stupid—"

"You got ripped off. That's a crime. It wasn't your fault." She leaned forward and pulled the get-back-to-work sign out of Nicky's hand. "You should have called us. We would have helped."

Finally she dared to look into her sister's eyes. She saw worry there. And love. So much love that it broke her heart. "I was on the East Coast, and you'd already loaned me so much money just to get through school. I couldn't call again. Especially since I had a friend whose couch I could crash on, but she wasn't in town right then. I had to wait until she got back. Besides, I had a job. I was going to get a paycheck soon enough. If nothing else, I would have moved into a hotel." She smiled, and the motion was easier than she expected. In fact, she was breathing a little better right then. No fear of a panic attack at all.

"You lost everything?" Her sister's voice was soft and filled with pain. "Is that why you took this job? Because it was back in Chicago?"

Nicky frowned, sorting through her memories of that time. "It paid the best," she finally said. "But yeah. I remember thinking that if the worst happened again, at least I'd live close enough to sleep on your couch and not a friend's."

"Oh hell, Nicky. I didn't know."

Nicky took a breath, letting her shoulders pull back down with the motion. "It's done with. I've paid back my loans and even have a decent cushion in my bank account. They even caught the asshole, not that I ever saw the money again." She opened her hands. "It's over," she repeated.

Susan shook her head. "I don't think so." She turned

the sign back so that Nicky could read it—Career first. Get back to work. "You talk about missing the signs— well, this is another one. This is the sign of a life out of balance. You say the past is over, that you have a good cushion."

"I do—"

"But you live in fear. This whole office, this career, all of it. It's a huge monument to your fear."

"That's not true!" she cried, but inside she was beginning to wonder.

"So you're not afraid? Which means you're purposely choosing work over roses? Your 401k over your goddaughter?"

"Of course not—"

"Stop talking, Nicky." Susan pushed herself to her feet. "Just think about what I've said. About your life. Meanwhile, I have to get back home to your former goddaughter."

Nicky jumped out of her own seat. "You're still firing me? But—"

"Stop talking! Start thinking!"

Nicky buttoned her lip, but she didn't like it. Meanwhile, Susan's expression softened a little. Not completely, but at least Nicky could still read love there.

"Yes, I understand now what happened to you. But that doesn't mean you're a good fit as godmother. You've got to think about your choices. About why you make them."

"But you can't fire me!" Nicky shot around her desk, trying to hold on to her sister. To hold on to her family. But Susan just shook her head.

"I love you, little sister, but you need a serious wake-up call. Don't spend the best years of your life on something that can't love you back."

"My job isn't about love, Susan."

"Exactly," she said. Then she gave her a tight hug before rushing out the door.

19

WHEN THE THURSDAY NIGHT amateur show was over, Jim once again got a ride from his brother, though not because he was too drunk to go by himself. Truthfully, he just liked his brother's company. After the bizarre week he'd had, Rick's quiet presence was just what he needed. Unfortunately, Rick's silence ended the moment they left the freeway and entered the subdivision.

"So she's given you the big kiss-off."

Jim didn't bother answering. He'd already explained about her career and the e-mail that said they had to delay things for the moment. There was no point in belaboring the point again when they both knew it was the big kiss-off.

"Don't worry, bro," Rick said. "I get the feeling you'll be seeing her a lot sooner than you think."

Jim frowned at his brother. "Enlighten me, Obi-Wan."

Rick pointed ahead as he rolled down the street toward Jim's house. There in his driveway sat Nicky's Pontiac Sunfire. Jim sat up straighter, trying to see if she was sitting on his porch.

Rick sighed. "You are one lucky bastard, you know that?"

"I don't assume anything where Nicky's concerned."

"Wise man," Rick drawled, but Jim barely heard him. He was already out of the car and striding up the driveway. Sure enough, there she was on his porch just like last time. Except that she didn't have that vague look in her eyes. And she absolutely didn't stand up and take off her blouse.

Instead, she barely lifted her chin, and her eyes never met his. She just sat there hunched. She didn't even seem to notice that her skirt was crushed awkwardly beneath her, and her suit jacket lapel was flipped the wrong way. Jim's chest tightened in terror. Clearly, something really bad had happened.

"Nicky? What going on?"

She still didn't meet his eyes. "I got fired."

"You're kidding!" The thought sent him reeling. "After all the hours you put in? I can't believe it. What morons they are!" He dropped down beside her and tried to gather her into his arms. She went easily, her body listless. He pressed his cheek into her hair and tried to think of something to say. Sure, nobody had died, but her job was everything to Nicky. Her sense of security, along with her sense of self. To lose that would be like dying to her.

"It's all my fault," she murmured. "I don't blame her in the least."

"Don't be ridiculous. They're idiots to fire you. You work harder than anyone else I've ever known."

"Yeah," she said as she rolled farther into his embrace. "That's the whole problem."

He frowned. "You got fired because you work too hard?"

She nodded.

"Nicky…" He lifted her chin. Again she moved listlessly, as if all the fight had gone out of her. That more than anything else terrified him. "Nicky, you know you're more than just your job, don't you? I know this is a shock right now, but you'll get a new job in no time."

She frowned and some of the spark returned to her eyes. "What job? Why do I need a new job?"

He blinked. He wasn't drunk, but maybe the beer was affecting him more than usual. "That's a good idea, Nicky," he said slowly. "Take this time to rest a bit. Focus on yourself for now. Job hunting can wait until—"

"What are you talking about?" she asked, straightening. Then her eyes abruptly widened in understanding. "No, no! I wasn't fired from my *job*."

He blinked. "Um, then what—"

"From my family," she said in a miserable wail. "I was fired from my family."

He almost choked on his surprise. He knew that wasn't polite—this was clearly devastating. But… "Family can't get fired, Nicky. And even if they could, yours would go through hell and back for you."

She shook her head. "No, they won't. That's what I mean. I was fired as godmother. I forgot the meeting with the priest. Again! I don't blame her."

Jim began to understand. So, finally her workaholic life was catching up with her. He pressed a kiss into her forehead and then tugged on her arm. "Come on. Let's go inside and talk."

She arched a brow at him. "You sure you want to risk

it? I mean, I was in the middle of doing the slow dump with you. I wouldn't blame you if you didn't want to invest—"

"Just shut up and come inside, will you? No one's dumping anyone tonight."

"Except for my sister," she said. Then she rubbed a hand over her face. "Gawd, I sound like a whiny child."

He dropped a quick kiss on her lips, forced himself not to linger there, then tugged her upright. A moment later, he had his front door open and was gesturing her inside. He tried hard to keep his mind out of the gutter, but when she stopped and stared at the heel marks on his hallway wall, his mind went straight south.

"Wow, this has been a weird couple of weeks," she said softly.

"Yeah," he agreed. Then his breath caught as he stared into her eyes. He could see it right there—an unspoken longing—and his body hardened in response.

"Maybe you could just hypnotize me into being a better sister."

He swallowed and looked away. "I don't think I'm that good."

"You are," she murmured as she stepped forward. Her hand touched his chest. She slipped her fingers beneath the buttons on his shirt and thumbed them open.

He grabbed her wrist, forcing himself to stop her. "I can't do this, Nicky."

She froze. "What?"

"Don't you see what's happening? The hypnosis, the sex, it's all just a way of turning off your brain when life gets too hard."

She stilled, her eyes pulled wide. And then she crumpled. Her eyes filled with tears and her hands went to cover her face. "Oh god, I'm awful!"

He laughed—gently—then tugged her into his living room. Less than an hour ago, he'd given up hope for more with her. For much of anything with her. But now, with her right here, his heart felt lighter than it had in over a week.

"It's not like I complained, Nicky. And I'm still a guy. If you really want mind-obliterating sex, you just give me a call."

She shook her head. "But that's the whole point, isn't it? That's why you did the whole pizzeria family date. You want more. My sister wants more. You all *deserve* more. And I…" Her voice cut off and she looked away.

"Don't stop now, Nicky. You what?"

"I don't have more to give!" She slumped as she dropped down onto his couch. "I don't want to end up at sixty looking back at all the spreadsheets I've done. But…"

She was staring at her hands where they were clenched in her lap. He settled next to her, extending his own hand over hers. "But?" he prompted.

"But that's all I'll ever have because I can't find room in my life for anything extra. People are going to start giving up on me. Susan already has." She sighed and flipped her hand over in his. "And those who are sticking around…I push away."

He waited a moment, trying to consider his next move. She was here, but it was only because of another crisis in her life. How did he make it so she would stay forever?

"First off," he said, "I'm not going anywhere. I pushed

too hard, too fast with that pizzeria date. I didn't ask you what you wanted, I just pushed."

She sighed and squeezed his hand. "Yeah, but I was the one who freaked. I...uh...I do that a lot lately."

He narrowed his eyes, his mind catching her phrasing. "Have you had more panic attacks?"

She nodded. "Just one. After I decided to not call you."

He arched a brow. "Wasn't that a clue that you should absolutely pick up the phone?"

She shrugged. "Yeah, but my boss called me into a meeting while I was still recovering, and...well..." She let her head drop onto the back of the couch. "And Susan thinks I make all my choices out of fear."

"Well," Jim began, choosing his words carefully. "You do realize what words trigger your hypnotic state, don't you?"

She frowned for a moment, then she closed her eyes with a groan. "You're safe with me. You can trust me. Wow. Couldn't get more obvious than that, could you?"

Unable to keep from touching her, he stroked a hand across her cheek. "It's no crime to be afraid. And I like that I make you feel safe."

"And I can trust you. I know that."

"But you don't feel it, do you? Not unless I hypnotize you."

She shook her head. "It's not that simple." Then she shrugged. "Or, hell, maybe it is." She looked into his eyes. "I feel safe with you. I always have, even back on prom night. And once I feel safe, there's no holding back on—"

"On a sexual level," he said, his heart sinking. There it was, as baldly stated as possible. Everything they had together was based on "safe Jimmy." But he didn't want to be just her safety net. He wanted so much more. And while he was deciding what exactly he wanted to do about that, she started speaking.

"Did you know I used to be a marathoner?"

He frowned, trying to follow her jump in topic. "Um, should I? Was it in high school?"

"No, college. Freshman year. I was feeling fat so I started jogging and I liked it. Then jogging became running, which rapidly became marathoning. I met a guy and we would run for hours together."

He blinked, annoyed by the surge of jealousy for this unknown runner. "Are you saying you want to take up jogging again?"

"I can't. I tore my ACL during my first real race." She abruptly pushed up from the couch to begin pacing. "Don't you get it? I went from nothing to marathoning in a few months. Then wham, torn ACL, and that obsession's over."

He shifted on the couch. He could see that the word *obsession* was key.

"And then there was my glorious career as an eBay antiquer. Do you know what the markup value is in antique dolls?"

He shook his head.

"My aunt gave me one as a present while I was laid up from my knee surgery. But the doll had a sister, so I decided to buy it on eBay. And then I found out what the value of the whole collection would be, and I started searching everywhere for it. I was on an extremely limited budget, but that made it all the more fun. I spent all my time watching antique doll auctions and calculating the value of my collection."

He blinked. One of his neighbors collected figurines

of odd children with sappy expressions. Her entire house was littered with them. He just hadn't expected that Nicky would be one of them.

"Go ahead. Ask me where my collection is now."

"Um, where is your collection?"

"Sold off. It was about the only thing that asshole left me, but even before that it was stored in a pile of boxes. It wasn't the dolls, it was the competition. The deals. The winning!" She pumped her fists in the air right in front of him, and when he just stared at her, she abruptly became self-conscious. She straightened, her hands dropping to her sides.

"The rest you know," she said softly. "I graduated, got my job and…"

"And now your obsession is your job, career advancement. You do it to the exclusion of all else."

She nodded and turned away from him. "It's what I do. I've never done things by halves. Even…fear. It just…consumes me. Except when I'm with you." She dropped to her knees before him, looking up into his eyes. He saw fear in there, just as she'd described. But he also saw a wealth of strength she just didn't seem to recognize.

He touched her face. He wanted to kiss her, but he held himself back. "You're stronger than you realize."

She shook her head. "Not without—"

"I'm not going to hypnotize you again." He said it sharply, before he even realized his intent. But it was the truth. "I—I won't be your crutch. Not that way. I want…" He sighed, knowing exactly what he wanted from her. A relationship. A life together. But would they have the chance to build one if he never hypnotized her again? He didn't know, but despite everything, he couldn't just be her sex toy.

She smiled. "I was going to say not without *you*." She took a deep breath. "It has nothing to do with the hypnotism, Jimmy. I just feel safe with you. Which makes it easy for you to put me under, but the lack of fear... that comes first. And that comes from you."

He was silent for a moment, studying her closely. She was feeling lost right then and completely overwhelmed. Good, he realized, with a small amount of shock. The pieces were falling into place in his mind.

"So you're not afraid with me. But it's more than that, isn't it? You need boundaries. To keep you from being so obsessive. And you need a safe environment in which to explore those boundaries without getting hurt."

She nodded, her eyes huge. "I have that with you. Assuming the fear doesn't overwhelm me and I shove you away."

"But that's why you like bondage. Because you can't run. Because you're forced to be with me."

She winced and her face reddened, but she didn't respond.

He leaned forward, putting it all on the line. He knew what he had to do—he just had to find the balls to do it. "But can you be with me without the hypnosis?" He leaned to the side table and popped open a drawer. Then he pulled out a pair of handcuffs and held them right before her eyes.

She reared back. "Jimmy?"

"Can you, Nicky? Can you submit to the bondage, can you *enjoy* it without the excuse of hypnotism?"

She frowned at him, but her nipples tightened. "Yes, of course I can."

"Hold on. There's more." He took a deep breath. In for a penny, in for a pound. "You have a lot of passion, Nicky."

She rolled her eyes. "That's never been in question. At least not around you."

"Passion, not just for sex, but for life. For work, for family, for everything. But no one can do everything all the time, so you channel it, focus it. And that leads to doing one thing all the way, all the time."

She huffed. "That's what I've been telling you. Obsessive."

"Which is why you need someone else to help re-direct you. Why you need someone to tie you down and make you think of something else. Or not think at all."

"Hence the hypnotism and bondage. I know. I get it."

"Hear me out. You need help setting boundaries. The handcuffs are just one way you manifest that need. I think I can be that man for you. I think I can help balance your life. But only if you'll let me." Then he opened the cuffs. "These are metaphorical, Nicky. But will you do it? Will you surrender to me without the hypnosis? Of your own, free, fully aware will?"

She stared at him, and he could tell she was think-ing deeply. Her breath was short. Not quite panting, but certainly faster than normal. But was it from anger or arousal? Or something else?

"One last thing," he said.

She arched her brow when he didn't immediately continue.

"I, um, I think I'm falling in love with you. That means I want it all with you, Nicky. Maybe not right away—certainly not all of it right away—but I want marriage, kids, a life together. If you don't see that hap-pening with me, then don't torture me."

He was so busy pushing his words out that he didn't

immediately see her reaction. All he knew was that she went completely still while her eyes remained riveted to his. It was almost as if she was under hypnosis again, except he knew she wasn't. She was very aware of what he was asking. He just didn't know how she was going to answer.

Then she slowly reached forward and drew the cuffs out of his hands. He held his breath, not daring to break the moment.

"You really think you can help me set boundaries? You can help me balance my life?"

He nodded. "If you'll let me."

"And you'll be patient with me? You won't let me shove you away? Because you're falling in love with me?" Her voice broke on those last words, but he answered as calmly as if his life and his heart weren't on the line.

"You'll always be safe with me, Nicky. I won't hurt you. And I swear to god I'll do everything I can to keep you balanced and sane." He realized he was using her trigger words. It was an accident, but he was terribly afraid that she was about to say no.

Unfortunately, he could see now that she wasn't going to hypnotize so easily. Even saying she was safe with him didn't produce that vague blissed-out state in her anymore. Which meant he was screwed. She wasn't going to go for it. She wasn't—

Click.

He looked down. She'd snapped the cuffs onto her wrists and was looking at him with her sex-kitten eyes. "What now, Mr. Magic Man? How are you going to help me now?"

20

NICKY'S HANDS SHOOK as she looked down at the cuffs on her wrist. Jimmy loved her. Or was starting to love her. Her heart squeezed painfully in her chest. She wanted him to love her. She wanted that so much because…

Her mind stuttered with the thought, but she pursued it. She chased it down and grabbed hold of it with both hands. Perhaps he was exactly what she needed. Perhaps he was the man who would change everything for her. She could trust him to help balance her life. She could trust him to help her see everything more clearly. God knew she was doing a piss-poor job of it herself.

"Nicky?" he said, his voice tight with worry as he looked at her face. "You're looking all terrified again."

"Perhaps," she whispered loud enough for him to hear, "perhaps I'm falling in love with you, too."

His whole body reacted. His eyes were so intense, his gaze felt like a laser on her skin. His hands jerked forward, but he stopped them halfway to her face. He took a step closer, too, but he did it slowly. Then he gently caressed her cheek and mouth, the touch so exquisitely tender that it brought tears to her eyes.

"Nicky," he said softly, but he didn't continue. Then, before she could process his words, he abruptly reached down and flipped her over his shoulders.

"Jimmy!" she gasped. One moment she was standing there, the next she was over his shoulder with her head flopping down by his delectable rear end.

"There's something that's been bothering me," he said as he started climbing his stairs.

"Yeah?" she said, though it was hard from this position. With his every step, she felt the powerful bunch and release of his muscles. Damn, he'd come a long way from his scrawny nerd stage.

"That first night you told me your fantasy. About nipples and…well, coming from just nipples."

She flushed. "Um. Yeah, well…"

"Well, nothing. I didn't do it right that night. I was drunk and all, and—"

She pushed up as best as she could. He had made it to the top of the landing and was heading down the hallway. "It doesn't matter."

"It sure as hell does," he said. "Plus, it bothers me that we've never done it in a bed."

She didn't speak again because he was dropping her down on his bed. The noise she made was more of a gasp than a word. His shoulder remained in her belly, though, as he was using his body to hold her down. While she was pushing the hair out of her eyes, he was crawling down her legs and doing something with her feet.

Click.

"What—?"

He straightened. She looked down and was stunned to see that her ankles were handcuffed together. Where had he got another set of cuffs? She grimaced as she tried to move her legs apart, but there was no give. None at all.

"I know it's tight," he said, "but it's the only way I'm going to keep on task and not cheat."

She blinked at him, the reality a bit much to process. "You cuffed my legs together?"

He nodded, his grin growing almost sly. "And I'm going to tongue your nipples until you come."

"But…" she gasped. Not that it didn't sound good, but she wanted to feel him inside her. She wanted real thrusting, grinding, squeezing him until he screamed. Not just…

He leaned forward to nip lightly at her lips. "You're going to trust me, remember?" Then he pushed her onto her back.

She went without complaint, mostly because he was bigger than she was and with her legs cuffed tight together she didn't have a lot of leverage to fight him. He made short work of her blouse, opening it and popping off her bra with sure movements. Good thing it had a front clasp. Then she felt it: his hands on her breasts. Wow, he was good. The lift, the stroke, then the thumbing caress over her nipples. Yes! God, yes!

"Jimmy, undo the cuffs. I want you inside me."

"Nope," he said as he leaned closer.

He tongued her nipple. He teased it, he nipped it, he sucked it in. She was gasping at the exquisite feel. The tension was building, her blood was simmering, but it wasn't going to be enough. He was nuzzling beneath her breast, licking while she struggled not to moan. It was great. It was beyond great. But she was never going to finish this way.

"Pistachio," she gasped. "Undo me so we can do this right."

"This is right," he said against her breast. Then he flipped to the other side. "And this is left." He nipped at the tip and she bucked beneath him.

"Really, Jimmy. Pistachio!"

"Trust me, sweetie. You agreed to trust me completely." Then he returned to her nipples. One hand on the left, his mouth on the right. Twisting, stroking, sucking. It was all fabulous, but it wasn't what she wanted. It wasn't him between her legs. It wasn't...

He lifted his head and his eyes caught hers. His expression was serious, his face gentle despite the intensity of his gaze.

"I'm not falling," he said as he squeezed her nipples. "I've fallen."

She frowned. Her mind couldn't keep up with the sensations he evoked. She was panting and her breasts felt so sensitive. "What?" she gasped.

"I have fallen in love with you. I love you."

She stared at him, her breath suspended. He loved her. She could see it in every line of his body. He hadn't stopped what he was doing, but his eyes were what consumed her. Dark. Mesmerizing. And so filled with love that she fell right then and there.

"I love you, too," she whispered. Then the wave hit. One long, orgasmic roll of ecstasy. Her body arched into it, her breath hitched on a gasp, but she never broke eye contact with him. She loved him. And he loved her. They could work out all the rest later.

Five minutes—hours—aeons later, the contractions eased, the bliss faded, but the love remained. She was still handcuffed, but she was able to lift both hands to his face and stroke him. God, she loved touching him.

"Jimmy," she murmured as her mind began to return.

"Yes?"

"That was the perfect orgasm."

Epilogue

NICKY SUCKED IN as she zipped up the back of her cheerleader costume. Okay, so she couldn't find their actual high school colors, but at least she could get into the outfit. Turned out a regimen of regular sexual play was pretty helpful in keeping trim, despite all the pistachio sundaes she'd eaten in a year of dating Jim.

And tonight, in honor of their anniversary, she was going to give him his favorite fantasy. Apparently Jimmy still harbored fond memories of her as a cheerleader and him as the high school geek who finally gets the girl. She hadn't actually been a cheerleader, but this was his fantasy, so she played along. Especially since she didn't mind reliving the good parts of being a teenager, not to mention the real-life discovery that geeks make great lovers. Hence the new, easy strip-off cheerleader uniform.

Besides, she was also warming him up for her announcement. She'd decided to change up her life even more. Upper management was great, but she was still in plastics. She wanted something different, a new challenge in a field she really enjoyed. Given the strides she'd taken in her confidence, she now felt strong enough—without fear enough—to take the risk and send out résumés. But first she had to crown her decision, so to speak, with a fantasy night.

Twenty minutes later, she was pulling into his drive-way, pleased to see the lights on in his house. He'd just come back from a business trip to New York, where he was selling yet another brilliant engineering idea. Something about redesigning a water processing de-vice that cut the cost of filtration by forty-three percent. She didn't know anything about engineering—or water filtration, for that matter—but she was pretty sure she could figure out the business incentive to buy his idea.

She ran up to the door and rang the bell, her heart already beating fast. She had a key, but it was way more fun to start in character from the beginning. She'd even tied her hair back in a ponytail just so she could bounce it a bit when she spoke.

The door opened and she was speaking before she really took in the sight of him.

"Hi there, is Jimmy home? I've got a problem with calculus before…" Her voice trailed away as she looked at him. His hair was mussed, his eyes had bags and he was wearing ripped jeans and a greasy tee. "Um…wow. Problem in New York?"

"What?" He rubbed his hand over his face. "Wow, Nicky. Nice outfit."

She put on her most vacant expression, complete with a ponytail flip. "Whatever do you mean, Jimmy?"

He grinned, grabbed her by the ponytail and hauled her inside. It was awkward. She stumbled a bit over his front door, but he caught her. Then he pressed her hard and fast against the wall. Their kiss went from zero to infinite in less than a second, and she let herself arch into his groin. Thin cheerleader panties allowed for so much interesting friction against jeans.

A half hour later, she was naked and stretched halfway up the staircase. He had collapsed beside her, one hand still toying with her ponytail.

"I swear," he murmured into her hair, "next time we'll make it up to the bedroom."

"I'm not complaining," she answered as she pressed a kiss into his chest. She wanted to do a little more, but she was still very aware of how tired he seemed. Which probably meant bad news. "So what happened in New York?"

"Hmmm?"

"New York," she said as she shifted to look up in his face. "But we don't have to talk about it, if you don't want to. I'm here for you whatever you need." She couldn't resist wiggling her hips just a little bit. "However you need."

He groaned in reaction and pulled her in for a kiss that didn't go deep enough. "I am so freaking lucky to have you in my life," he said when they separated. "Thank you."

She lifted herself on one elbow. "Don't you have that backward? Shall we recap a bit of the changes in the past year? When we first...um...hooked up last year, I was a middle manager having a nervous breakdown. I worked all the time, had alienated all my friends and was working on completely disconnecting from my family when, wham, in comes the Magic Man."

"No pun intended," he drawled.

She blinked, momentarily thrown. "Oh. Comes. Haha. But shut up, I'm on a roll here."

He dutifully pressed his lips together.

"You magically removed my phone, gave me amazing sex and forced me step by step into a life. A real life."

He shook his head. "You made the changes, Nicky. You would have done that without me."

"Or crashed because I was e-mailing while driving and died horribly." She straightened enough to flick him with her ponytail for speaking when he was supposed to be quiet. "So now, one year later, I'm upper management at much bigger salary while working less hours. Yes, I got the promotion because of my brilliant reorganization that saved a ton of jobs, but without you, I would have buried myself in the promotion, too. But I didn't and now I go to movies, have hot fantasy sex and discovered I like rock climbing. I'm even a godmother to a beautiful little niece, and thank you for smoothing things over with Susan."

She touched his face, trying to impress on him how integral he was to her life. "I couldn't have done any of it without you. I feel like a whole person because of you. I love you."

His expression remained playful, but his eyes were serious. He understood what she was saying. "Let's not forget who I was *Before Nicky*. I was just as much a workaholic as you, but without any focus or drive. I was locked in this garage creating magic illusions and playing Magic Man whenever my brother had a hole in the Thursday night lineup."

"I like the Magic Man!"

"But he isn't an engineer. If I didn't have the example of your drive, I would never have thought of my new water filtration design."

"You would have gotten to it eventually."

He shook his head. "I don't think so. You have such

focus, Nicky. It inspires me." He waggled his eyebrows. "In more than one way."

"Love that inspiration," she drawled. Then she touched his chest lightly. "So what happened in New York?"

"Oh. Yeah. They bought my design. And for a ton of money."

She brightened. That was the exact opposite of what she'd expected. "But that's wonderful!"

"Except there's a catch. I've been up all night working out the details. That's why I wasn't ready when you showed up."

She frowned. "A big catch?"

He nodded. "Yeah, they want me to run their R & D department. In New York."

Her heart crashed. Her whole body crashed, but her mouth apparently still worked. "New York?"

"Yeah. It's a great opportunity. They're working on projects that…" His words spun on, outlining everything he would get to do, the people he would work with. And when he slowed to take a breath, she pressed a kiss to his lips, though her heart was breaking. "It's time for me to start working with people again. In an R & D department. There's so much more inspiration when it's not just me."

"So you're moving to New York."

"Not yet, I'm not. I told them I had to think about it. It's a big change."

"But do you want the job?" she asked, even though she could already tell the answer. He was practically vibrating with excitement. She couldn't take that away from him, even though he would be leaving her. And she would again be stuck alone with a not-so-fulfilling job of her own.

"Yes," he said softly as he lifted her chin. "Yes, I do, but I told them I'd have to ask my wife first."

She blinked. The tears were making her vision fuzzy and apparently clogging her ears. Had he just said wife? "You're married?"

He laughed and pressed a kiss to her mouth. "Not yet, I'm not." Then he reached down through the railing to pick up his discarded jeans. Pulling a jeweler's box out of his pocket, he got down on one knee before her. As they were still on the stairs and were both naked, it was an odd sight, but she didn't care. He was beautiful. Absolutely beautiful.

"Nicky Taylor, will you do me the greatest honor and marry me?"

She swallowed. "Are you…um…are you proposing because you want me to go to New York with you?"

"I'm proposing because I love you, Nicky. I always have. But this past year has been incredible in so many ways. If you want to stay here in Chicago, then I'll stay. If you want to work in Paraguay, I think I'd go just to be with you. But I'm hoping you want to go to New York with me. There are a ton of corporate jobs there. You'd be snatched up in—"

"Yes! Yes yes yes yes yes!" She threw her arms around him and nearly toppled them off the stairs. He stabilized them with one arm on the railing. That was perfect because it gave her the opening to kiss him as deeply as she wanted. And she definitely wanted.

He slowed her down after a moment, pulling back enough so he could slip the ring on her finger. She stared at it a moment, then lifted her gaze to his. "I want to go to New York, Jimmy. I was going to tell you that I've decided to quit my job anyway. It's time to shake things up, to try something new."

"Take all the time you want to find something new. My salary will more than cover what we need."

"I love you, Jimmy."

He straightened, excitement and desire alive in his face. She knew because she felt it, as well. Alive and happy and so excited about the future that she could barely breathe.

"I love you, too, Nicky."

"But I have one requirement," she said sternly. "The Magic Man and his toys come, too."

He arched his brows and she could already see his mind working. "You want me to hypnotize you again? Shall I put a spell on you?"

She laughed. He didn't know that he'd gotten hold of her a long, long time ago? And in all the best ways possible. "Nah," she drawled as she reached down and gripped him. "I want you to teach me how to control you."

"Sweetheart," he groaned. "You learned that a long time ago."

This time they made it to the bedroom. And the garage. And all the way—eventually—to New York and a very wonderful life.

* * * * *

Harlequin Intrigue top author
Delores Fossen presents
a brand-new series of breathtaking
romantic suspense!
TEXAS MATERNITY: HOSTAGES
The first installment available May 2010
THE BABY'S GUARDIAN

Shaw cursed and hooked his arm around Sabrina.

Despite the urgency that the deadly gunfire created, he tried to be careful with her, and he took the brunt of the fall when he pulled her to the ground. His shoulder hit hard, but he held on tight to his gun so that it wouldn't be jarred from his hand.

Shaw didn't stop there. He crawled over Sabrina, sheltering her pregnant belly with his body, and he came up ready to return fire.

This was obviously a situation he'd wanted to avoid at all cost. He didn't want his baby in the middle of a fight with these armed fugitives, but when they fired that shot, they'd left him no choice. Now, the trick was to get Sabrina safely out of there.

"Get down," someone on the SWAT team yelled from the roof of the adjacent building.

Shaw did. He dropped lower, covering Sabrina as best he could.

There was another shot, but this one came from a rifleman on the SWAT team. Shaw didn't look up, but he heard the sound of glass being blown apart.

The shots continued, all coming from his men, which meant it might be time to try to get Sabrina to better cover. Shaw glanced at the front of the building.

So that Sabrina's pregnant belly wouldn't be smashed

against the ground, Shaw eased off her and moved her to a sitting position so that her back was against the brick wall. They were close. Too close. And face-to-face.

He found himself staring right into those sea-green eyes.

How will Shaw get Sabrina out?
Follow the daring rescue and the heartbreaking
aftermath in THE BABY'S GUARDIAN
by Delores Fossen,
available May 2010
from Harlequin Intrigue.

HARLEQUIN® *Blaze*™

is proud to present

New York Times bestselling author

Vicki Lewis Thompson

with a brand-new trilogy,
SONS OF CHANCE
where three sexy brothers
meet three irresistible women.

Look for the first book
WANTED!

Available beginning in June 2010
wherever books are sold.

---

red-hot reads

www.eHarlequin.com

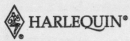
LAURA MARIE ALTOM

The Baby Twins

Stephanie Olmstead has her hands full raising
her twin baby girls on her own. When she runs
into old friend Brady Flynn, she's shocked to find
herself suddenly attracted to the handsome airline
pilot! Will this flyboy be the perfect daddy—
or will he crash and burn?

Babies
&
Bachelors
USA

REQUEST YOUR FREE BOOKS!

2 FREE NOVELS PLUS 2 FREE GIFTS!

HARLEQUIN®

Blaze™

Red-hot reads!

HARLEQUIN® *Blaze*™

is proud to introduce...

New York Times bestselling author

Brenda Jackson

with
SPONTANEOUS

Kim Cannon and Duan Jeffries have a great thing going.
Whenever they meet up, the passion between them
is hot, intense...spontaneous. And things really heat
up when Duan agrees to accompany her to her
mother's wedding. Too bad there's something
he's not telling her....

Don't miss the fireworks!

*Available in May 2010
wherever Harlequin Blaze books are sold.*

red-hot reads

www.eHarlequin.com

HB79542